ANYTHING BUT ORDINARY

ANY
THING
BUT
ORDIN
ARY

LARA AVERY

HYPERION
NEW YORK

alloy**entertainment**

Produced by Alloy Entertainment
1700 Broadway, New York, NY 10019

"Upgrade U" by Angela Renee Beyince, Shawn C. Carter, Willie James Clarke, Sean Garrett, Garrett R. Hamler, Beyoncé Gisselle Knowles, Solange Knowles, Clarence Henry Reid, Makeba Riddick (Angela Beyince Music, B day Publishing, Carter Boys Music, EMI April Music, EMI Blackwood Music, Inc., EMI Longitude Music, Hitco Music, Janice Combs Music, Solange MW Publishing, Team S Dot Publishing, Yoga Flames Publishing). All rights reserved.

"La Vie En Rose" by Mack David, Edith Giovanna Gassion, Luis Guglielmo Guglielmi (Universal Polygram International Publishing, Inc., Warner Bros, Inc. (Warner Bros Music Division)). All rights reserved.

Adventures of Huckleberry Finn by Mark Twain (pseudonym of Samuel Langhorne Clemens). All rights reserved.

Printed in the United States of America

First Hyperion paperback edition, 2013

10 9 8 7 6 5 4 3 2 1

V475-2873-0-13196

Designed by Liz Dresner

ISBN 978-1-4231-6450-0

Visit www.un-requiredreading.com

SUSTAINABLE FORESTRY INITIATIVE

Certified Chain of Custody
Promoting Sustainable Forestry

www.sfiprogram.org
SFI-01054

The SFI label applies to the text stock

To my brother Wyatt

Farewell, hello, farewell, hello.

—Kurt Vonnegut, *Slaughterhouse Five*

PROLOGUE

Most divers forget to see the space, the air. You focus on your body—how to make it into a thin board, or curl it up like a piece of spaghetti and flatten it back out. You lift off and you barely have time to think before you hit the water.

But Bryce, she would never forget where she was going when she was about to jump. She would never forget the small eternity between the stone platform and the deep blue below.

"Bryce Graham," reporters asked her, "only seventeen. What's your secret?"

She would usually say something easy, something written on an inspirational T-shirt. "Concentration," she would say. "Focus." Things that should be said into microphones. But never: "Fear, Ted. Fear."

That day, Bryce was carried up the stairs by the noise of the crowd. They yelled louder for her than for anyone else. This was her home, after all. Those were people from her high school in the stands, though she didn't know most of them. The Tennessee fans wore little clothing and were red in the face, yelling and yelling. The out-of-towners wore Olympic Trials T-shirts and fanned their pale faces with programs. One of them had become as red as anyone in Nashville, on account of the heat. He had gone to the concession stand for a soda, a Coke in a sweating plastic bottle.

He watched from his spot at the back of the building, propping the exit door open with his foot. He sipped his Coke, and a cicada landed on the bleachers. The crowd went silent as Bryce crouched at the end of the platform, like a cicada herself.

Bryce jumped. She was bending, coiled, and the insect rubbed its legs together, calling out to any other cicada that might be nearby.

She was bending, coiled, and the man from out of town felt the breeze on his face.

She was bending, coiled, in the small eternity between block and blue.

She was only seventeen. What was her secret?

Space, Bryce answered, but there was less than she thought, and her tight twist was an inch longer than it should have been, and the inch happened to be on the curve of her lovely head. Her skull jutted over the cement platform, and the weight of her body went falling, falling into the empty Tennessee air.

If you asked Bryce's mama how long was a cicada, she would answer, "About one inch," and if you asked her daddy, it'd be the same answer. Bryce Graham's sister, too, and her friends. Nashville people.

If you asked that man from out of town, he wouldn't know, but he could hear it calling out into the air, the moment before a plume of blood colored the pool dark red.

CHAPTER ONE

Heartbeat has been generally faster."

Who said that? Match sound with image. Lights and metal and movement. A woman's hands untying something. Sounds but no image. Try again.

"Get her records," a voice said. "She's coming—" Before the sound cut out again, the light pooled, brighter and brighter.

This was a game Bryce played. How long would it take for the endless exhaustion to set in? Sometimes she bothered to open her eyes, but it was difficult enough just to remember that she had been around once, being and talking. The very idea made her retreat back into the dark. It hurt to be alive.

But she had been playing sound-plus-image for a while now. Five days? Five hours? Even if it was five minutes, the sensation was a strong one.

Someone's breath was on Bryce's face. "Get her parents on the phone."

Bryce's parents. She had heard their voices in the darkness, but she could never make out their words. They had touched her shoulder, rubbed her forehead. But Bryce was too tired. *I can't,* she tried to say. *I can't move.*

"Bryce."

Bryce could tell by her tone the woman was trying to speak softly, but she wanted to put her hands over her ears. Her fingers twitched at her sides. She opened her eyes. Light flooded into her skull. Colors became shapes, shapes became people.

The smells and sounds switched on like a machine. The acidy scent of cleaner, mechanized humming, metal creaking. A gray-haired woman leaned over her with a stethoscope, blocking the fluorescent lights.

She was awake.

✳

"I'm hungry," Bryce had breathed, though it was a pain to talk. The room was silent, save for the beeping of machines and the slurping of liquid Jell-O from a straw. She moved her tongue through the sweet substance, relearning the motions of every swallow. The movements were blurry, but everything else came at her with an edge. The hospital room was the beige color of pale skin and seemed to throb. Her mother sat near the bed in an electric-pink bathrobe. Her father stood next to her mother, in his same old gold-and-black Vanderbilt sweat suit, COACH emblazoned on the chest. Their faces erupted in teary smiles as her gaze hit them.

It was all different. Her mother's hair was shorter, for one. And her dad had lost some weight. They had been waiting for a long time. What had happened?

"Bryce." The voice from earlier, now softer, came from a short-haired woman in a white coat. "My name is Dr. Warren. Do you know where you are?"

"Hospital," Bryce said in a dull monotone that didn't sound like her voice. She cleared her throat. "Hospital," Bryce repeated in a higher, lighter tone, looking at her parents.

Dr. Warren kept writing on her clipboard. "Do you know what you are recovering from?"

Bryce swallowed. Her throat felt like sand. She could do this. *Push yourself.* "I was asleep."

Dr. Warren nodded. "You were in a coma. You suffered serious head trauma. In order to heal, your brain eliminated your consciousness for quite some time."

The dive, Bryce thought, the blinding crack coming back to her in a flash of pain. The memory replayed itself again as Dr. Warren spoke, and for a strange moment Bryce could see herself from the stands, a blur in a colorful swimsuit, falling to the water.

"The good news is that your brain's healing progress was not as absent or slow as we had thought. We'll do some more MRIs, but it looks like your cognitive functions will continue to improve."

"Why can't I move?" Bryce asked. Beside her, the heart monitor began to beep more quickly, as if warning her. As if her body knew something she did not.

"Your recovery depends on how well your muscles return from extended disuse," Dr. Warren replied carefully.

Recovery. Her brain was foggy, but the word never meant much to her. She avoided injury. For competitive athletes, there was *could* or *could not*. There was no *recover*. She looked at her hands. They didn't move much, but they looked fine, a little pale and thin maybe.

"How long was I asleep?"

Dr. Warren looked at Bryce's mother, her eyebrows raised in a silent question. Her mother nodded at Dr. Warren. The doctor started in slowly. "Bryce, you've been unconscious for a while. Some things have changed."

Bryce felt blood rush to her cheeks. She ignored the doctor's steady gaze, trying and failing to clench her fists, feeling for the first time the presence of tubes stuck in her forearm.

"Where's Sydney?" Bryce's curly-haired twelve-year-old sister was probably taking advantage of her stay at the hospital that very moment, going through her stuff, putting on her junior prom dress and pretending she was a Broadway star.

"Your sister is out," her father said, crossing his arms.

"Out?" Bryce responded. "Doing what?"

"Syd—well." Her mother tightened the tie on her pink bathrobe. "She's . . . gotten older. We all have, even you." She laughed a little.

Bryce noticed the circles underneath her mother's light blue eyes, the gray glinting in her dad's close-cropped hair. They hadn't answered her.

"How long—"

She was interrupted by fast footsteps, the squeak of the handle, a bang on the wall as the door flung open. A tall, pale teenage girl loped in. She looked familiar.

Bryce's mother sprung up. "Not now." She stood between Bryce and the girl.

"Yes, now! Are you kidding?" the girl responded.

"Please," her mother said, but it was more like a command.

From the other side of the bed, Bryce's father said loudly, "Elizabeth—just . . ." He finished his sentence by shaking his head.

The girl wore fishnets and heavy-soled boots. Bryce glanced at her parents, but their eyes were fixed on the floor. Back to the girl. Dark waves. Their father's big dark eyes.

Sydney. The girl was *Sydney*. Bryce's heart skipped a beat.

Her mother stood over the chair. "Please. She's not ready. She's disoriented."

"Seriously, Mom," Sydney said through gritted teeth. "Maybe now would be a good time to pretend I'm part of this family."

Dr. Warren moved toward the door. "I'll give you all some time."

"Bryce." The girl grasped the support poles on either side of the hospital bed, as if the sight of Bryce made her dizzy. The smell of cigarettes filled Bryce's nose. She frantically looked for the dark freckle near Sydney's ear, the one Sydney pretended was an earring. It was there. "You're . . . awake," Sydney whispered.

"How—" Bryce began but stopped when Sydney looked straight at her, mascara streaked on her round cheeks. "How—how old are you?"

"Me?" Sydney landed her black fingernails on her chest. Bryce noticed for the first time a small hoop piercing her lip. "I'm seventeen."

Seventeen.

Bryce felt like she was underwater, trying to swim to the surface. She'd been asleep for five years? She was . . . twenty-two?

"Oh, my god," Bryce breathed. Her blood was pumping so hard it felt like it was trying to escape her fingers. Tears leaked out from her eyes, running down her face. She thought of her calculus exam, the one she'd barely studied for. Olympic Trials. Graduating from Hilwood High. She was supposed to stand next to Gabby. They'd planned it. Greg would be at her other side.

What now?

She couldn't look at anyone, though they were all looking at her. She closed her eyes.

Bile welled in her throat, and heat grew on her forehead, stabbed by pinpricks of pain. The hospital window was imprinted on the back of her eyelids, the world outside of it changing from night to day, and in another moment she felt the room was bathed in moonlight and sunlight, dusk and dawn.

A hospital room. The shades drawn.

Bryce realized she was looking at her own sleeping form on a strange, distant afternoon. Her family drifted around the hospital bed, looking like they used to. Her mother's eyes were glazed, as if they had been emptied of tears. She lay her head on the bed next to Bryce's body. Her father paced the room, his coaching whistle around his neck, anxiously running a hand through his dark hair. Sydney was still twelve years old. She sat in the patterned chair in the corner, her head in her hands, her body shaking silently. Nobody moved to comfort her.

Then the pain that had risen up so quickly vanished, and Bryce was blinking into the glare of the fluorescent lights. Her family stared back at her, still shadows of the people she knew. She wished this older, sadder version of her mom and her dad and her sister would go away and come back as their usual selves. With a pang she thought of their faces as she had last seen them, flushed and beaming above GO BRYCE! T-shirts. She had huddled with them in a big group hug. Her dad reminded her to watch the timing on her back tuck. Her mother told her to loosen her goggles, that they looked too tight.

Then Greg and Gabby jumped in behind her, and they were all smiling nervously at each other, their heads close together. Gabby reached to give Bryce's face a couple of playful slaps. "Focus!" she cried. Greg stretched across the huddle and his lips met hers in a soft, sweet kiss.

It felt like yesterday, not five years ago.

She'd awoken from nightmares before, but . . . the Jell-O rose up in her stomach as she realized she would never wake up from this.

This was her life now.

"I can't believe you guys," Sydney said, grabbing the arms of her chair. "Why doesn't she know that already? Why didn't you tell her?"

"Sydney, your input is unnecessary right now." Their father fumbled for his wallet. "I'm getting one of those crappy coffees," he muttered and walked out of the room, their mother following, talking in a low whisper. It was the first time they'd so much as moved since she woke up.

Sydney scooted closer to the bed. She continued to stare at Bryce in disbelief, as if at any moment Bryce would disappear.

"Have they told you anything that happened?" she slurred.

Bryce stared. "Sydney, are you *drunk*?"

"Did they tell you about everything?" Sydney pressed on. "About Greg and Gabby?"

"That's enough," Bryce's mother's voice came sharply from the doorway. She handed her coffee to Sydney. Bryce kept her eyes on her sister, begging her to go on.

"Bryce just woke up," her mom said in a gentler tone. She sat on the bed, crossing the long legs Bryce had inherited. She brushed hair from Bryce's eyes. "You must be tired."

"The opposite." Her body was heavy, but everything else felt flurried now, like snowflakes that were scattering away, and her mind was scrambling to catch it all. She wanted to move, but instead only her eyes darted, looking at Sydney. "Do Greg and Gabby know I'm awake?"

Her mother reached out to touch Bryce's cheek. "Let's just slow down."

"I agree." Dr. Warren had reentered, flipping a page on her clipboard. "Though her vital signs are excellent, with the extraordinary amount of cerebral activity that has occurred in such a small amount of time, Bryce is at risk for any number of brain malfunctions."

Bryce tried to meet her family's eyes, to show them somehow she was ready to wake up. For good. She wasn't a piece of faulty equipment breaking down, *malfunctioning*. She was here. She was back.

Dr. Warren put her hand on Bryce's shoulder. "Bryce, you've been amazing through all of this. You're really strong. But we don't know what's going to happen in the next few days, or even in the next few hours."

Bryce barely heard. She wondered when Greg and Gabby

were going to come. Were they really twenty-two years old? Was she really twenty-two years old? This was the last place she'd wanted to be in five years. She should have won at least one gold medal by now. Instead she was caught in a strait jacket of her own body.

"My one commandment is rest," Dr. Warren went on, her voice more relaxed. "I know it seems silly, but the best thing is sleep. Okay?"

"Got it," Bryce said, but her thoughts were elsewhere. Every second, more was coming back. Her nerves had faded, and all that was left were hard truths. She couldn't move her legs. That needed to change. I've got to get going, Bryce thought. I've got to get back to normal.

"Say good night, everyone," Dr. Warren continued. "You can sleep in the waiting room if you like. We'll be watching her closely."

Bryce's father leaned down to kiss Bryce on the cheek. "Good night, sweetheart. We'll be right outside."

"See you in the morning," her mother said, reaching down to do the same. Then she whispered in Bryce's ear. "You don't know how wonderful it is that I get to say that."

"Night, Bry." Sydney backed out of the room awkwardly.

Dr. Warren was the last to leave, smearing her makeup as she rubbed her eyes. "Get some rest."

Bryce wished she could lift her arm to wave. They were sandbags, heavy at her sides.

The door swung open, letting in a sliver of fluorescent light from the hospital hallway. The beam of light widened into an arc across the floor as Dr. Warren paused at the entrance. Then she closed the door, muffling the noise of the hallway and leaving Bryce alone in the dark.

CHAPTER TWO

Graham, Bryce. 3B. Neurology Wing. Vanderbilt Medical Center. Nashville, Tennessee. Third window from the right, if you're looking up at the glassy blue side of the building. Third from the left if you're looking out from that particular room, counting each window. Which Bryce was doing. Thirty-two, so far. Graham, Bryce. 3B. Heart rate normal. Blood pressure normal. Eyesight—blocked by a hopping cicada, trying to pass through the pane. Bryce followed the fluttering insect with her nose against the glass, making little pools of mist with her breath.

You don't want to get in here anyway, little guy. The cicada finally landed, inches from her cheek. Its long, bean-sized body looked like it was covered in armor. Its wings were like lace. Slowly, *slowly*, she picked up her hand from where it rested on the sill and brought it to the window. As her fingertips got closer, the glass got hotter. Not hot in a way that burned her, but warm and bright at the same time. She withdrew, wondering. Suddenly, the glass was liquid, melting away with light at the edges, and there was a hole big enough to reach through. The cicada stayed where it was, frozen like a bug in amber.

She put her hand toward the glowing gap and curled her fingers around the insect. She had it! Bryce brought the cicada back through, feeling its wings flap against her palm. She held it close to her face.

A flash of heat, and a blink, and it was gone. There was no melting or glowing. She was leaning against the window under the fluorescent buzz of room 3B, clutching at nothing.

"Weird," she said aloud. She looked around to see if anyone was watching, and then she tried it again, moving her fingers slowly toward the glass, but they hit the cool pane with a thud.

Bryce turned her wheelchair away from the window. She had been awake for a few weeks now, and as time went on, it became clear: something felt different, and not just about her; a filter colored everything. It was like at the optometrist's office when he flipped lenses in front of her eyes through a machine and asked her which one was clearer. *Number one, or number two,* he would say, but there were no blurry circles now. Each circle was clearer than the one before, crisp with the most precise details.

It was probably cabin fever. Anyone would start seeing things when their sights were limited to beige linoleum and cheesy paintings of waterfalls and castles. Bryce was surprised she hadn't started talking to herself. Apart from her family, she hadn't had all that many visitors. She had wanted to see Gabby and Greg immediately, but she got a visit from Elena, Gabby's mom instead. She told her they were backpacking with a group of their friends around Europe since graduating from Stanford. *Why Stanford?* Bryce had wanted to ask. Vanderbilt had offered them all scholarships. They hadn't even been thinking of West Coast schools before the accident. Now they were across an entire ocean. She wondered idly if there were any places to go cliff-diving in Europe. She had always wanted to do that.

There was a knock on the door. "Come in," Bryce said as her nurse, Jane, held open the door for an older man in a sport jacket. He was either a reporter or a doctor. She had already lost track of how many magazines and medical journals had interviewed her. She had told her parents to approve everyone who asked for an interview because the Grahams often got paid for the stories, and even though Bryce's parents refused to talk about it, she knew her treatment must be costing them a fortune. Her mom's design business had taken off in the last year, and her dad was still coaching at Vanderbilt, but it couldn't be enough.

Bryce ran her hands nervously through her hair in case he was going to take a photo, trying to remember who he was.

"You okay then, corncake?" Jane asked as she backed out the door.

"Well, um—" Bryce started, but Jane's Garfield-printed scrubs were already disappearing out the door.

"Hello there, Ms. Graham. My name is Dr. Felding." She shook his warm, dry hand. He was barrel-chested and balding. He looked like a coach, Bryce thought. "I'm the head of research for neurology at Cornell."

Bryce just smiled thinly, tuning him out. She had already answered a million questions from researchers at Columbia and Johns Hopkins. At this point, doctors across the country knew her brain better than she did. Apparently not only was her waking up after five years a miracle, her ability to talk and scoot around made her some sort of medical phenomenon.

Bryce had a hard time feeling miraculous when most of the conversations she had in the past month revolved around who was going to cut her toenails or walk her to physical therapy twice a day. She envied Sydney, breezing in and out for her obligatory five minutes a day at the hospital, wearing short skirts, smelling like the outside. Bryce did not feel like a miracle. She felt like a freak of nature. She felt bored.

The doctor was still talking. ". . . so I was hoping we could schedule a further evaluation at our facility, once you're up for travel."

Bryce just shrugged. "We'll see," she said, gesturing to her wheelchair, as if it might make the decision for her.

"So, Bryce." He took a seat on the chair next to her, taking out a notepad. "What was it like to wake up?"

"Like being dipped in a bucket of ice water," she began. This was her go-to response.

"Could you hear and see right away, then?"

Bryce recalled the lights pooling above her, the sounds of machines kicking in. "I could. It took a little bit—"

"Unbelievable," Dr. Felding interrupted in awe. "According to your charts, you are recovering more rapidly than any other documented case. And your journal mentions that you've even stood up a couple of times?"

"You have my journal?" Bryce's stomach twisted. It was

just a notebook in her now scratchy, second-grade handwriting that Dr. Warren told her to keep, so she could remember new skills that came each day, or side effects of certain medicines. But still. It was hers.

Bryce tried to glance behind the doctor, hoping Jane might come back.

Dr. Felding waved a hand. "Just a copy."

"Excuse me," a young man's voice said from the doorway.

Bryce's eyes were drawn to a pair of worn New Balance sneakers. The shoes were attached to a pair of khakis, followed by an untucked button-down shirt. They belonged to a handsome, dark-haired young man. The doctor's coat he wore seemed out of place.

He said sternly, "Are you authorized to be in here?"

"Hi. Liam Felding, Cornell University." Dr. Felding stood up and took the young man's hand. "I'm just asking Bryce a few questions."

"That's nice," the guy said dismissively, crossing his arms. "But visiting hours are over. She needs to eat lunch."

"The receptionist said until three o'clock," Dr. Felding protested.

"Blood relations only during lunch," he replied. Bryce thought she could see a hint of a smile on his face, but she wasn't sure.

"But——" Dr. Felding began.

"Are you her uncle?"

"No, but——"

"Her distant cousin?"

"No." Dr. Felding stood awkwardly.

"Kindly leave until she finishes lunch."

"How long will lunch last?"

The young man shrugged. "Could be forever, who knows?" This time, he glanced at Bryce, his eyes glinting.

Dr. Felding stared. The guy in the doctor's coat stared back. Finally, Dr. Felding closed his notepad and left.

"Thanks," Bryce said, as soon as he was out of earshot.

"I'm Carter." He crossed over to her; she took his outstretched hand. His eyes were a familiar blue-gray. Bryce felt the room drop away around her. They could have been shaking hands anywhere. In a park, in an elevator. Had they met before?

"Bryce," she said, and they let go.

"Bryce Graham, I am aware." He smiled. Then he said slowly, "I have to say, it's a trip to see you up and about." He turned to retrieve a tray from a cart outside the door.

"I never know how to respond when people say things like that," Bryce said to his back.

"It's just nice to hear your voice, I guess, after watching

you for so long." He attached a tray of chicken nuggets and mashed potatoes and peas to the chair's arms. "That sounded creepy," he finished, crossing his arms decidedly, as if stating a medical fact.

"It did, yeah." Bryce nodded and matched his tone. She had to laugh.

"I'm sorry. I'm a med student at Vanderbilt." He gestured behind him, as if the school was there. "I've been volunteering here since I was an undergrad—I see a lot of patients come and go. And sleep." He cleared his throat. "Anyway. I'm happy for you."

"Thank you," Bryce said.

Carter gestured to the tray. "Jane said, and I quote, 'Tell her if she doesn't clean her plate in fifteen minutes I will tan her hide.' So I would get on that."

He took a paper checklist out of his back pocket and put a mark next to her name, flipping the pen back behind his ear when he was done. Bryce took a bite and struggled to think of something to say. "So what year are you in med school?"

"Just my second year." He came back toward her. He tapped the folded paper on the back of her chair. "Can you keep a secret?"

Bryce nodded.

"I'm not actually supposed to be wearing a white coat."

Bryce pointed at him, her mouth full of food. "I knew it!"

He shrugged, and smiled. "Yeah, you don't get a coat here until you do a residency. But I saw you were on your own, and . . . well, I thought the doctor might not listen to me in my current ensemble," he glanced down at his khakis and untucked shirt, "as professional as it is. And then the supply closet was open. . . ."

Bryce found herself grinning. "Now that I'm keeping your secret you have to do something for me," she said, sticking rows of peas on her fork.

"What's that?"

She gave him a tentative look. "You wouldn't happen to have your laptop with you, would you?"

As time had passed and Bryce had begun adjusting to the big things, she started wondering about the little ones—what had happened to her Facebook when she went under? She had five years' worth of ESPN and SpringBoard posts to catch up on. She'd thought about asking Sydney to sneak in her phone, but the rare times Syd visited she was usually fighting with their parents, anyway.

"I do have my laptop." Carter looked at her, deliberating. "But they restrict anyone with high risk of brain overstimulation from computers. All the flashing and visual stimuli can give you a killer headache."

"Damn," Bryce muttered. She was getting antsy to do something besides stare out the window, counting tiles and imagining magical bugs.

"Wait there," Carter said suddenly. He turned on his heel and disappeared from the room.

"I'll try not to go anywhere," Bryce called sarcastically.

He returned minutes later, plopping what had to be a foot-high stack of magazines on the bed.

"Courtesy of the waiting room recycling bin," he said with a flourish.

Most of them were from the past few years. Dates she'd slept through slipped past her on the top corners, underneath them names and photos she didn't recognize. The glossy, blocky font seemed to invite her personally to discover THE BEST MOVIES OF THE YEAR, WHY NOW IS THE HOTTEST TIME FOR FASHION, and the CUTEST CELEBRITY BABIES. It was almost like Gabby were right there gossiping with her, catching her up on what she'd missed.

"Looks like you're going to be occupied for a while," Carter said.

"Yeah," Bryce said. "Thank you . . . so much."

"No worries," he said, backing out into the hallway.

"See you tomorrow?" she asked, suddenly. "I mean, in case I need you to scare away some more neurologists, or something?"

"Sure." He nodded and then he was gone.

She dipped her finger in mashed potatoes, and started to flip through the highlights of the last few years. Skirts getting shorter, then longer; computers smaller and flatter; starlets moving in and out of the spotlight; athletes getting caught with steroids and mistresses. Bryce was secretly glad Carter didn't include anything with actual global events. If the world was just made up of shallow celebrities and makeup tips, nothing had changed in five years. Everyone, everything, was just waiting for Bryce to wake up.

CHAPTER THREE

Is our car wheelchair accessible?"

Bryce sat between her parents in Dr. Warren's dusty, fake plant–filled office. She wore jeans and a tank top, as she had for the past week, to make it very clear that she would no longer be needing a hospital gown. She would no longer need to take her clothes on and off for stethoscopes, wires taped to her chest, and fMRI scans. It had been two months since she opened her eyes in April, and she was ready to go home.

Bryce's mother rubbed her daughter's back absently as she looked at one of Bryce's used copies of *OK!* The thrill of old magazines had faded fast, and Bryce had moved on to crossword puzzles. She greeted Carter every day with the challenge to find a three-letter word for *fasten metal teeth* or to *fill in the blank of 1970s Scorsese thriller,* ___ *Driver*. Because his head was filled with the Latin names for diseases, Carter was pretty miserable at pop culture. Bryce wasn't great either, but thanks to her dad's various collections, she was a wiz at most movies and music made before 1980.

Her mom looked up at Bryce's question and sighed. "No, it's not. It's just an SUV." After a moment, she said sweetly, "When it's time, we'll get one of those vans for you."

Bryce wanted to scream, *It* is *time!* but instead settled on, "I won't need a wheelchair soon."

Her father looked at his watch and made a noise of approval on the other side of her. Bryce could smell his aftershave. "Thatta girl. Did you read those articles about core strength I printed for you?"

"Yeah," Bryce said excitedly. "I've been doing the medicine ball twists, they've got me sore, but that's always a good thing, you know?"

He moved to the edge of his generic waiting room chair, like he was poolside at a meet. "I bought this DVD, too, about plyometrics. Maybe you can use the bars. Work on your quick-twitch muscles."

In the first couple weeks, Bryce and her dad had been hard-pressed to find things to talk about. While her mother fussed over things like getting Bryce a proper haircut, her dad just stared around the room. But then he attended one of her physical therapy sessions, and by the end of the forty-five minutes, he was informing the trainer about the best way to strengthen Bryce's genetically weak ankles. Maybe the world thought Bryce's insanely fast recovery was a miracle, but Bryce liked to think it was also the work of Coach Mike Graham.

Dr. Warren entered, her short gray hair in sweaty clumps, her white coat folded over her arm. "It's hot out there," she said.

Bryce cracked her knuckles and gave a small smile. "I wouldn't know."

"Sorry," the doctor said, nodding hello to Bryce's parents and settling behind the desk. "It's been a while. How are you?"

Bryce moved her wheelchair back so she could stretch out her legs on the carpet.

"Bryce?" Bryce's mother touched her elbow lightly.

"I'm great." Bryce gestured to her straight legs. "I feel like I've been doing pretty good."

"You've been doing excellently. Your patterns are relatively normal, save a few glitches."

Her father jumped in with pride in his voice. "She was standing up and sitting down at her evening session yesterday. No help from anyone. She even took a step on her own."

"I think I'm going to walk without assistance pretty soon," Bryce said.

Dr. Warren raised her thin eyebrows. "That's a lofty goal."

"I agree," her mother said, her eyes meeting Bryce's dad's. Bryce's mother turned coolly to Dr. Warren. "I think my husband forgets that she isn't his little workhorse anymore."

"It's her goal, not mine," he said quietly. "She wouldn't rest if I asked her to."

"He's right," Bryce let out. She felt her mother stiffen beside her, but she had to say it.

Her mother tucked her blond shaggy hair behind her ears and folded her hands over her khaki Bermuda shorts. "Dr. Warren, I think I am completely justified in wanting to keep my daughter's recovery slow and steady. There are risks, are there not?"

Bryce rolled her eyes.

"There are risks, yes. We'll get to them momentarily. . . ." Dr. Warren said, shuffling the contents of Bryce's file. Then she looked up. "Tell me, Bryce. How's your memory?"

Bryce's heart began to beat faster, and she felt her face get hot. Her mother's gaze hit her from her left, her father's eyes from her right.

"Bryce, how is your memory?" Dr. Warren asked again.

"F-fine," she stammered.

Her memory was more than fine. Her vision was, too, but Bryce didn't know how to talk about that. It had to just be a side effect from her eyes being closed for so long. She looked at a planted tree in a corner of the office, noticing each vein crisscrossing the dark leaves. She could trace the green veins back, through the flesh of the leaf, to where the branch split the bark open. She shouldn't be able to see it like that all the way from her chair, as if the tree were under a microscope. Bryce tore her eyes away, focusing instead on the doctor, but it was no use. The wooden patterns on Dr. Warren's desk were impossibly clear. She should tell them. But what if they thought something else was wrong? Her mouth went dry.

Dr. Warren furrowed her brow and leaned forward again. "Bryce, you're giving real short answers here. I don't want to have to keep telling you this, but it is very, very important you tell me every detail of your progress."

"I am."

"You've experienced nothing out of the ordinary? Nothing at all?"

Bryce opened her mouth, then closed it. She envisioned the endless rounds of tests, the wires taped to her forehead, the incessant beeping of monitors following her every move, her every thought. Bryce shook her head. "Nothing."

"I am trying just as hard as you to make this—"

Bryce crossed her arms. "You guys have been watching me for years. What else do you need?"

"They're just doing their job, honey," her father said calmly.

Dr. Warren leaned back in her chair, sighing. "We're not inside your head, Bryce. We can monitor and record all we want, but we can't explain what your brain has done to wake itself up. It's very . . . complicated."

"What's so complicated?" Bryce asked with disbelief. "I'm awake! The end!"

"Your brain was most likely aroused by some sort of stimulus. Or rather, some sort of reception of outside information that it perceived as stimulus. Any stimulus that's strong enough to bring you out of a coma puts you at risk for seizure, aneurysm, stroke. If we don't know exactly what areas of your brain are being used, we are not going to know what to do when it . . ." Dr. Warren trailed off. Bryce swallowed but did not look away. "*If* it functions abnormally one day," she finished, her tone more measured.

"Do you understand what she's saying?" her mother turned to Bryce.

"My brain's been normal since the minute I woke up," Bryce said stiffly, ignoring her mother. "I don't know what else I can do to convince you guys."

Bryce's mother took her hand. She put her face close to Bryce's so Bryce couldn't ignore her. "Baby, this is for you, this isn't for me." She squeezed her hand hard. "Of course I want you to come home. But you heard what could happen."

Bryce looked into her mother's blue eyes filling with tears. She felt her gut wrench.

"I've been awake for two months, and we still don't know what's going to happen. I don't really see the point of me being here if we're just going to sit around not knowing. Why can't we 'not know' at home, where I'm happy?"

Dr. Warren cut in. "The more we observe, the more we know. We can't observe you there."

Bryce had to laugh. "That's kind of the point."

Dr. Warren shook her head.

Her father cleared his throat, glancing at his wife then back to the doctor. "For the record, I also think Bryce should stay, and she knows that."

Bryce put her head in her hands.

"But—" he said quickly. Bryce looked up. "I can assure

you, if you do release Bryce like she wants, we will be dedicated to her recovery to the utmost degree. We will be vigilant about her medication and her training."

Dr. Warren smiled wryly. "I don't doubt that."

"Please." Bryce snatched the file off the desk and flipped through the pages. "You have enough. Please. I have to see if I can get back to normal."

"Well." She held out her hand for Bryce's file. Bryce handed it back to her. "I can't say we didn't anticipate this. You've been asking to go home every day since you woke up." She looked at Bryce. "If you decide to discharge, there's nothing I can do. You're legally an adult. But as your doctor I am telling you, as I have told you numerous times, it's in your best interest to stay."

Bryce's heart beat wildly now. *If you decide to discharge* was a phrase she had never heard before. The words lingered, hanging in the air.

Before Dr. Warren could clarify, Bryce sputtered, "I decide to discharge!"

Dr. Warren smiled. "It doesn't quite work like that." Her seriousness returned. "Your condition is stable, but there's no way we will let you leave without maintaining an attentive record of how you're doing. I will expect you to come in for evaluations."

"Fair enough." Bryce suppressed a smile and shrugged.

"Well, then. Let's pull up the paperwork." Dr. Warren held the door open for Bryce's parents, her father loping behind her mother.

While her parents got the car, Bryce wheeled to the front desk. Her legs were twitching with impatience as Dr. Warren wrote out prescriptions and schedules.

"Hey," a voice said behind her. She turned to see Carter, who was wearing an enormous backpack. He smiled wide at her, his eyes crinkling in the corners. Freckles dotted his cheeks.

"Guess what?" Bryce almost shouted. Before he could say "What?" she squealed, "I'm going home!"

"Oh," he said, looking surprised. "Right now?"

"Right now. I don't even have to wait for a van. My parents are going to try to fit my chair in the back of their SUV."

"Well, hot damn," he said, feeling for the pen he always kept behind his ear. He looked a little crestfallen but managed a smile. "The neurology wing is going to be so boring without anyone demanding obscure trivia from me."

"You're not going home for summer break?"

"Ha," he let out. "No such thing as summer break in med school."

"Sorry," Bryce said, smiling. "But at least everyone is going to get their lunch faster."

He hesitated for a moment, then ripped off a corner of the sign-in paper and scrawled his number on it. "In case you ever need anything. Five letter word for *underneath* or whatever."

"Below." Bryce smiled.

"Give your parents my best."

"There they are," Bryce said as a large black vehicle pulled up in front of the outpatient doors.

Carter got behind her, pushing Bryce across the lobby. Since she'd gained the strength to use her chair, Bryce had dismissed anyone who wanted to wheel her around like an infant. But Carter had done it without a word, and though she could hear his sneakers padding across the floor, he seemed to barely be there.

The midmorning light swept in through the automatic doors, opening and closing for people coming and going. Bryce put her feet on the rests of her chair, and let herself enjoy the sensation of being led into the sun.

CHAPTER FOUR

Bryce sat back in her seat as the sycamore trees whizzed by the windows of the SUV. Each tree and house and lamppost left a swirl of color as they drove past, like the trail of a painter's brush. She looked away, trying to savor the feeling of coming home. Though she'd never admit it, she was tired. Tired of the fuss it took to do anything besides sleep, tired of the smell and taste of anti-bacterial everything, of being surrounded by stainless steel.

The buildings of Nashville had scattered to make way for rolling pasture that rose up before Bryce's eyes like bread baking, and she felt the road change from pavement to gravel under the tires. They were in her neighborhood. She couldn't wait to collapse on the giant corduroy couch in her living room and drink some lemonade out of the plastic Vanderbilt cups that passed for stemware at the Grahams'.

The car finally slowed, and Bryce's vision was filled with her big blue house, the stone pathway up to the door seeming to float in the lawn like lilypads. It was beautiful and different in her new way of seeing, but just that it was still there was enough. Her father set up the wheelchair near the curb. Sydney stood outside the door in bare feet and an enormous T-shirt with the Muppets on it, looking half asleep.

"Sydney!" her father called. "Take Bryce to her room. We'll go get everything set up inside."

Sydney latched on to the chair and wheeled Bryce down the hill in the back of her house, toward the pool and the basement entrance. *Bryce's* entrance.

Bryce's room was the only bedroom downstairs, and on summer days she would leave the sliding doors open and blast her pump-up playlist from the speakers in the common room. She and Greg and Gabby would practice on the high dive, or take turns pushing each other into the water. Bryce smiled to herself. Her dad was always at the office, but when her mom was home, she would play Queen albums out of courtesy. *For god's sake,* her mom would say if hip-hop entered the mix, coming around the side of the house, her pale knees streaked with dirt under her gardening apron, *at least pick something I can sing along to.*

Bryce couldn't wait to see the bright blue of the pool. She had grown up as comfortable in the water as she was on land; before long, she was happiest in the air, the emerald lawns spilling out around her for miles. But as they came down the hill, she grimaced. The pool was full of bugs and sticks and leaves. The high dive was encrusted with dirt.

"There," Sydney said as they reached the back entrance.

"I'm so glad to be home," Bryce sighed, but as they wheeled through the sliding doors, she gasped.

The floor was covered in bright white tile, and the only places to sit were long, boxy shapes near the wall. In the corner sat a large black rectangle, hardly a chair, and where the antique grandfather clock had once been were vivid red platforms topped by black and white sculptures. Bryce felt like she was in the lobby of a trendy hotel.

"What . . . happened?" she stammered.

There was a moment of silence before Sydney looked up from her phone. "Oh, yeah, it's really different, I bet," she said, barely glancing at Bryce.

Bryce rolled forward, but it was not onto the rust-colored shag carpet. There were none of the tables with bowls of hard candy on them, or the vases of dried flowers she and Sydney picked for her mother when they were kids. This was not her basement.

"I wish someone had said something." Bryce took a deep breath, wheeled across the tile, and reached to open the door to her room.

The light was the same, hazed a little bit by the plants in the window wells. Dust swirled in the soft beams pouring in. Her trophies were gone from the dresser, and they'd taken down her John Wayne posters. A little part of Bryce expected her bed to be unmade like she'd left it. Her jeans to be on the floor. Her dirty dishes stacked on her dresser.

There was noise from upstairs—her parents were starting dinner. Bryce looked at her sister standing near the closet, turquoise fingernails tapping on her phone. "Well, at least there are no weird statues in here," Bryce sighed.

"Right?" said Sydney. She put away her phone as Bryce wheeled back toward the door. "Hang on," she said.

Bryce stopped.

"I just want to say this while Mom and Dad aren't, you know, hovering." Sydney looked down at her feet, twisting her shirt in her hands. "I'm sorry I was drunk when you woke up."

Bryce almost wanted to laugh at how much like the old

Sydney she looked just then. Like she was being forced to apologize for biting her sister.

"It's okay, Syd." She tried to smile reassuringly. "How often do you go out like that, anyway?" Bryce asked. She wondered every time she saw the dark circles around her sister's eyes, or smelled her smoky clothes when she entered a room. What was Sydney doing? Who were her friends?

"Oh god, not you too." Sydney stiffened. "I didn't know you were going to wake up that night, okay?"

"Chill, Syd. I was just wondering."

"Well, it's none of your business, pastor."

The look in Sydney's eyes told Bryce it was time to let it go. But who *was* this person gazing coldly back at her? She flashed back to the girl who had come home crying from her first middle school dance, the silky dress they had picked out together wrinkled, the mascara she'd "borrowed" from Bryce smeared. Bryce remembered stroking her soft hair as Syd explained, between sobs, how the boy she liked didn't want to dance with her. That felt like just a few weeks ago. Now Syd's face was hard. She didn't look like a girl who cried anymore.

"Hey, listen—" Bryce was going to ask her sister if they could just start over. Things had been off between them ever since she woke up. But Sydney had already turned back to her phone, making her way to the stairs.

"Look, I appreciate your concern and all," Sydney said, taking the steps two at a time. "But I don't need someone else telling me everything I do is wrong."

❋

Bryce wheeled around the front hall upstairs, feeling like a stranger. Like she should ask her mother for a tour, or something. Before, family photos had dotted the long entryway, as if introducing the house's residents in grand fashion as you entered. But the photos now sat on a circular table hidden in the corner. She wondered if anyone ever looked at them anymore. Her eyes landed on a familiar shot: a picture of her at her first diving meet when she was seven, her hair tucked beneath a cap and goggles, her father and mother hunched down next to her, beaming in matching T-shirts. But most of the photos were new. Sydney with braces, Sydney at the wheel of the van, and another that made her stomach drop—the three of them looking pale and cold, standing outside of the hospital with a Christmas wreath. Their faces were drawn and tired.

The sitting room, too, had been sleekly remodeled, modern paintings made of streaks and dots hanging where the old paintings of Mississippi barges had been. Only the den had remained the same. She touched the ratty orange sofa with a sense of comfort. She opened the top drawer of her father's desk, where he always kept the plans for the two-seater plane that he had been working on for years. They were there, rumpled from having been unfolded and folded a million times. And there was the small TV, a stack of DVDs on top of it. She and her dad would hole up here, watching tape together. She moved toward the pile of Vanderbilt diving-highlight DVDs, and paused. The last DVD was dated four years ago. She held it in her hand, a hard knot forming in her stomach. Why was there nothing more recent?

She didn't want to know, but she was afraid that she already did. It was a relief when her mom called her to dinner.

✱

In the kitchen, the Grahams sat facing each other on black, hard-backed chairs, eating Bolognese off of oversized white plates. The plates were so big, the food looked like dabs of paint.

"This isn't bad, Beth. You haven't made it this way in forever," her father said.

"Maybe because we ate takeout every night for the last five years," Sydney murmured, rolling her eyes.

"Mmm, gotta carbo-load," Bryce said, ignoring her sister. "Just like before a meet. I'm going to walk tomorrow."

"Bry," her mother warned. "You've had a lot of excitement, you don't want to push it."

"Sure she does," her dad chirped. Her mother stopped chewing. "Well, that's why she's progressing, Beth. Because she knows how to train properly."

Her mother gave a fake laugh. "Oh, that's right. I forgot you're an expert in physical therapy."

"Unlike you, I'm trying to encourage—"

"I'm done," Sydney interrupted, taking her napkin from her lap. "I have to go."

"No, you don't," her mother responded firmly. "You're grounded."

"Mom," Sydney said with a condescending smile, "we did the family dinner. Let's not try the whole punishment thing." And with that, she was gone.

Bryce looked at Sydney's empty place, her food untouched. The front door closed, and her parents continued to eat. Bryce opened her mouth to say something, but what?

"So . . ." She swallowed a forkful of pasta. "I went into the den before dinner. Are you going to tell me why the last highlight DVD in there is from four years ago?" Over the last couple of months, when her father came to her hospital room from work in the evenings, she had grilled him about how the season went, how his recruits were looking, how Vanderbilt had placed in their conference. But he had always changed the subject.

Bryce's father sighed and put down his fork. "I stopped coaching, Bry."

She thought of her dad's office in the Vanderbilt athletic department, where she'd spent so much of her childhood. The walls were so covered by Sydney's art and Bryce's newspaper clippings that the paint was barely visible. Bryce would sit in the swivel chair while he was at practice, eating granola bars and playing games on his computer. Then when she made the Junior Olympic team, he let her practice with the college divers. They would sit for hours after everyone else had gone home, watching tape, pointing out the good and the bad as Bryce iced her legs and braided her long, wet hair. She tried to imagine it now, filled with someone else's kid's drawings.

"It was . . . too much . . . after your accident, Bryce. I hope you understand."

"But you're still wearing Vanderbilt stuff—"

"Of course, of course. I didn't leave Vandy. Never could. I'm in Admissions now."

"So I guess we won't be watching tape, then," Bryce muttered.

"We can still watch tape," her father offered, trying to smile.

Bryce just shook her head. "You guys have to tell me

things." She found herself choking a little on the words. "I mean . . . I know you're not used to me being able to hear you, but I'm here now. I'm awake."

Her parents looked at each other, but their eyes never met, as if they were trying to press two magnets together at their north poles. They barely smiled, barely touched each other. Is that how it had been the whole time she was asleep?

Her father squeezed Bryce's forearm, and they went back to their pasta. Silence and chewing. The sipping of water.

The phone rang.

"I'll get it," Bryce said, wheeling to the kitchen, past her parents' protests.

"Graham residence."

"Oh, my god." The young man's voice sounded oddly familiar.

"Hello?" Bryce said.

"Bryce, it's Greg."

She clutched the phone, speechless.

"Bryce?" His voice had gotten so much deeper.

She leaned on the counter and hoisted herself out of her chair.

"Um. Hi." Why did her voice suddenly sound so high and squeaky?

"Hi," he said. She could tell he was smiling. She caught a glimpse of herself in the reflection of the window. She was, too.

A few days before her accident, she and Gabby and Greg had gone to Percy Lake, like they always did in the summer. They started at the back of the dock and then sprinted toward the lake, shoving off the edge in long jumps over the water, sailing, seeing how far they could get.

It was only a few days before trials, but for some reason Bryce wasn't worried about getting hurt. She had done a good one, a really long jump with a big splash, and she came up to the surface farther away from the dock than she expected. She swam back toward the shore, and Greg slid into the lake to meet her. They treaded water, facing each other, their long limbs scissoring in and out of cold patches in the cloudy water.

"I love you," he had said, smiling.

"I love you, too."

I love you, she heard again, as clear as if it was yesterday.

"I can't believe it's you. How are you?" he asked. He spoke slowly and earnestly, just like he always did. She had fallen for that drawl right away.

"Good question. It's been crazy—" Before she could finish, she heard another voice at the end of the line. "Who's that?" Bryce said.

The voice came closer to the receiver. "It's Gabby! Are you seriously on the phone right now? Is this seriously Bryce Graham?"

Bryce let out a scream.

Her parents rushed into the kitchen. She held out her hand. "Everything's fine, it's just Greg and Gabby."

Bryce's mother looked like she had seen a ghost. "But why are you out of your chair?" she whispered.

"Oh, Beth. She's fine. Let her talk to her friends." Her father turned back toward the dining room.

"Bryce!" Bryce heard Gabby yell even though the phone was pressed against her chest. She held up one finger to her mother and returned the phone to her ear.

She felt like laughing and crying. The last time they had talked on the phone, Gabby was contemplating cutting her hair because she had gotten her heart broken by Bryan Godard. She was going to start being tough, like Bryce. Bryce had pointed out that her own hair was long, and Gabby had forgotten all about the haircut idea by the next day.

"It's so good to hear your voice," she said now. Something missing for the past few weeks began to fill up inside her.

"God, Bryce, tell me about it!" Gabby squealed.

"Whe—where are you guys?" She stumbled over her

words. She had started to say, *Where have you been?* But that could wait.

"We just got back into town. From Europe! We went after graduation."

Bryce felt her forehead tense. "Wow, um, congratulations! So, are you—"

"Listen, Bry, Greg's phone is running out of batteries, and we know you need to chill with your family and stuff, so we're going to make this quick."

"Make it quick, then, Gab, geez," Greg said in the background.

"Point is, we're coming to see you! Tomorrow. Can you meet us at Los Pollitos for happy hour? I mean, can you, you know, go places?"

"I think so." She was twenty-two. She could do whatever she wanted. Right? "No, definitely. I can definitely go tomorrow."

"Awesome."

"I want to say bye," Greg said before coughing into the receiver. "See you, Bryce. It's so great you're awake. I can't wait to see—"

"We love you, Bry!" Gabby had taken back the phone.

"Wait," Bryce said.

"Ye-es?" Gabby cooed.

"What time—when is happy hour?"

"Officially, five. But we're gonna make it four." Gabby laughed and the connection ended, by hang up or dead battery, Bryce couldn't tell. It didn't matter.

She looked out the kitchen window above the sink to her dark backyard, seeing the faint outline of the barn in the distance. She smiled and ran her hands under the faucet. With a splash, she brought the lukewarm water up to her face. She wished it were tomorrow already.

"Tomorrow," she said aloud, loving the sound of the word. She had a whole lifetime of tomorrows now.

CHAPTER FIVE

The sunlight hit Bryce's closed eyes, forcing them open. She swung her legs over the bed and felt the cold tile with her toes. She set her feet on the floor. She braced herself at the edge of her mattress and pushed up. She was standing. But this time she didn't have a physical therapy bar to hold on to. Good, Bryce thought. If I can do it in therapy then I can do it here. She teetered a bit, held her arms out beside her, and took a shaky step. She took another one.

Bryce wove across the room, again and again, each step bringing back memories of the life she had left behind. Step: dressing Sydney up as a gold medalist for Halloween.

Step: getting ready for winter formal with Gabby. Step: long afternoons icing her muscles, her body feeling as if it were still in flight, slicing through the warm Tennessee air. She went on and on until her steps became more sure, each one steady and deliberate.

She was getting faster, and the smell of bacon was coming from the kitchen.

Now for the stairs.

＊

Bryce stared furiously at her greasy plate. "Come *on*, Mom!" She was starting to sound like Sydney, but her mother was being ridiculous.

Her mom responded by loading the dishwasher a little too roughly.

"You're not in any shape to be going out for *drinks*. I don't know what they were thinking."

"I'm not five years old, Mom. This isn't a playdate. They invited me to a restaurant. It's not a big deal."

"It *is* a big deal."

"Why?"

Her mother stopped rinsing dishes. She turned off the water, and straightened. She looked like she was about to say something more. But then she closed her mouth and reconsidered.

Bryce narrowed her eyes. "What?"

"Anything could happen, Bryce, and . . . well." She wiped her hands on a dish towel. "Some things you can't just shrug off."

"Nothing's going to happen."

Bryce's mother looked pained. "Did they mention anything . . . on the phone?"

"What? Why?"

"It's just, Bry . . ." She sat down at the table and looked at Bryce. "Some things have changed. For everyone. Even Gabby and Greg."

"Obviously, Mom. I'm—"

Just then, Sydney wandered into the kitchen with her eyes half closed, poured herself a full mug of coffee, and began to wander back out.

"Syd, wait!"

Sydney paused, not turning around.

"Do you have a car?"

"Does it look like I have a car?" She resumed her journey to her room. Then she called, "Cars are a waste of money at this point in my life. I just get boys to drive me around."

"How progressive of you." Bryce reached into her pocket for her new cell phone. She wished she had Greg's number so she could just get him to pick her up. But her only contact was Carter. Actually . . . "What if Carter came?"

Her mother turned around, thinking. Carter had met her parents during a few of their visits, and they liked him. He had a way of explaining Bryce's procedures to them so that everyone actually understood.

Bryce went on excitedly, "He could drive me to and from, and stay there just in case." Her mother considered her from the sink.

"It's just Greg and Gabby, Mom. They know me." Bryce was still met with her mother's stern face. What did she think was going to happen? They were going to hug her too hard? Make her laugh too much?

Bryce tried again. "You can trust them to be . . . you know, gentle."

Again, her mom stayed silent. She bit her lip. Finally, she sighed. "Fine. Call Carter."

*

As four o'clock approached, Bryce began to bite her nails. Sometime after breakfast she had returned to walking practice. She hated the idea of Greg and Gabby seeing her in a wheelchair.

She glanced at her reflection in her mother's full-length mirror, clutching the shelves on either side of the closet. Her hair used to be platinum from the sun, and went past her chest; now it was dishwater-blond and hung to her shoulders. Her legs had long ago lost their tan; now they were pale and a little pink. What used to be muscular calves were thin as toothpicks. Too thin under swollen knees and sore thighs. That's enough of that, Bryce thought, making a face, and she turned her back on her new reflection.

All that was left of Bryce's closet, buried deep in a corner behind some skis, were a pair of deep red cowboy boots her mother had bought her from a leather dealer at the Tennessee State Fair. They were Bryce's favorites, the leather so worn and molded to her feet that they felt like an extension of her body.

She threw them aside to put on a black dress from her mother's closet. Maybe that would make her look grown-up and serious. Her hand shook as she applied mascara. She stepped back and looked in the mirror. A long-lost member of the Addams family stared back. With a struggle, she took off the dress.

Maybe something more casual. She had managed to sneak some clothes from Sydney's closet. Sitting on the floor, she shimmied into a pair of her mother's yoga leggings and one of Sydney's oversized T-shirts that read PUNK IS DEAD. She squinted. She looked kind of like one of those washed-up celebrities just released from rehab that she saw in the gossip magazines.

God, who cared? Who cared what she wore?

Gabby did, that was who. She was always trying to get Bryce to borrow her clothes. But Bryce felt like she was playing dress up when she'd worn them, like Sydney trying to look "mature" in their mom's pearls and heels.

She sighed.

Gabby seemed to float through everything like it was nothing. If Gabby was the one in the coma, Bryce had a feeling she would have woken up speaking fluent French, or with a cure for cancer. She was better than Bryce in school, and she always wrote beautiful poems and essays about diving, like it was an art and not a sport. Gabby probably had the time of her life in Europe. Probably met some bullfighter in Spain and now they were in love. How was she going to talk to Gabby about any of this stuff? Bryce's knowledge of the world was limited to the diving platform and the neurology wing.

Finally, she chose a simple V-neck from her mother's pajama drawer and settled on a pair of cutoffs from Sydney's pile. And her cowboy boots. To make herself taller. To make herself the same height as Greg.

Could she kiss him right when she saw him? On the cheek

or something? She wondered about what her mom had said, that things had changed for Gabby and Greg. Maybe he was dating someone. Girls had always thrown themselves at Greg, like Rebecca from homeroom, who had lips like sausages. Or Rebecca's friend Kate, who called Bryce "man shoulders" behind her back. They made Bryce want to punch her desk, and then she would go home and lie on her bed, wondering why Greg wanted her when he could have anyone. But he brushed the Rebeccas and Kates off with a polite smile and made his way down the hall to lean against the locker next to Bryce, with a dandelion he had picked for her. She'd asked him once, why her? "Because you're special, Bryce. You can *fly*."

One of the silly, poetic things Gabby wrote about diving was that her best friend, Bryce, moved like the air when she was around water. That she was a completely different person on the platform, like some soaring, glorious creature. But Bryce might never climb up to the platform again. She'd never again fly.

Bryce walked out of her mother's room, trying not to lean on things, and glanced at the clock on the microwave. It was four. She grabbed her house keys, heading for the door. Her mother was still at the grocery store, and Carter would be here any minute.

She moved slowly to the entryway, clutching the wall,

and jumped when she opened the door, spotting a pair of navy New Balance sneakers. She looked up. Carter, wearing a plaid shirt, was raising his fist to knock.

He put down his hand. "You're standing."

"Hi, yes." Carter began to respond, but Bryce cut him off. "Sorry, but can we get going? I don't want to be late."

"How did you . . . I mean, that's remarkable."

Bryce made another sound of frustration.

Carter continued, drawing out his words, "Considering you recently came out of a coma."

Bryce looked past him to a tiny white Honda. "Is that your car?"

Carter followed her gaze. "Thar she blows."

"Well, it's a good thing I'm not bringing my wheelchair. That thing is tiny."

"First of all, it's fuel efficient," he explained as Bryce hobbled past him. "Second of all, your mother said I had to do a little checkup before we go—"

Bryce held up a hand. "My head is fine, my brain is fine, and my friends are waiting at a restaurant."

He wasn't budging. He took off his backpack, pulling out a doctor's kit. "It will take two seconds."

"You're being such a nerd right now," Bryce said under her breath, taking a seat on the porch swing.

"I could leave, you know," he said, attaching the blood pressure sleeve.

Bryce held her tongue. The sleeve pinched her arm, hard.

"Yep, could go at any time," Carter said softly as he held up a stethoscope to her chest. "Got plenty of other fun things to do. Mrs. Hidalgo likes it when I put the telenovela on for her in the afternoon, even if she can't exactly say so. And the bedpans always need washing, so . . ."

At that, Bryce burst out laughing, picturing the awful hum of the fluorescent lights and sickly smell of the neurology wing. Carter laughed, too.

Carter helped her down the pathway and opened the door for her. Bryce got in the car.

Carter turned over the ignition a few times. "I guess there's no point in convincing you to bring your chair."

"Nope. It's inside, where it belongs." Bryce tapped the dashboard. "Let's go!"

*

Ten minutes later, they pulled into the parking lot of Los Pollitos. "Is the food here good?" Carter asked, peering through the windshield.

"I don't know," Bryce said, opening the car door. "Thanks for the ride. I'll call you when I'm done." But before she could climb out, he was on the passenger side, offering her a hand.

He walked her to the entrance and pulled open the doors with their chili-pepper handles.

"Wait, you're coming in?" She turned to face him.

He stood, hands in his pockets, looking at her. He pursed his lips and shrugged.

Bryce took her hand off the door. "You don't need to come in."

Carter scratched his chin. "First of all, you can barely walk. Second of all, I am a free citizen and can go wherever I want."

She looked around. No sign of Gabby's or Greg's cars, or at least the cars they used to have. She *did* need help walking.

Then she heard Carter mutter behind her, "Third, I want nachos."

She laughed as he helped her through the open door.

CHAPTER SIX

The dimly lit restaurant smelled like spice and meat cooking. Laughter floated from the scattered tables. A mousy-haired hostess approached, smiling nervously. "Are you Bryce Graham?"

"Yeah," Bryce said, trying to smile back. "I'm looking for my friends? They're, um——"

"They're here. Come with me."

Bryce was almost putting her whole weight on Carter's forearm, but there was nothing much she could do about it. They followed the hostess through rows of booths, hearing Bryce's name murmured in low voices.

Bryce licked her dry lips. This was it.

Gabby and Greg sat shoulder to shoulder at an elevated table near the bar. Their heads were close together, as if they were whispering. They didn't see her at first.

Gabby was beautiful. Her black hair was out of its usual braid, flowing, and her features had become more refined, high cheekbones and large eyes, lips tinted with a darker color than her favorite bubblegum gloss. She wore a turquoise wrap dress and ballet flats. She was describing something to Greg with hand gestures, her face lit up.

Bryce let go and approached them in small, shaky steps. She waved to Carter slightly as he backed away somewhere. She was in another world now.

Greg had filled out, and his hair was longer. He nodded at what Gabby was saying, but didn't look at her. He stretched his arms behind his head and put them back down, rubbing his eyes with his palms. Gabby laughed, trying to pull his hands away from his face, shaking him to "Wake up!" Greg laughed with her, still rubbing his eyes.

Suddenly Bryce was standing right in front of their table. She tried to pull down her T-shirt over her shorts, but Gabby spotted her and screamed.

She leaped off her chair and wrapped her long arms around Bryce's neck.

"Hi, Gabby," was all Bryce could say.

She smelled the same, like shampoo and lavender, and Bryce wanted to go back to her room and lie on the floor while Gabby lay on her bed, talking up to the ceiling. *Why don't we talk like they did in the olden days?* Gabby used to sigh. *Like, then, instead of "please," they said "prithee." Prithee*, she would repeat, and laugh. *Prithee, prithee, prithee* . . .

Greg beamed at Bryce. She didn't have to think about whether or not she would kiss him, because he began his tight hug with his mouth on her cheek, and ended it with a kiss on the other. She felt his stubble between her jaw and her neck, his back muscles against her palm. He stepped away, putting his hand through his blond hair the way he always did when he was nervous.

"Oh my god," the three of them kept saying. "Wow."

When they finally sat at the small table, they had to laugh. The world had become their own for a few minutes, and now they were back in a restaurant, and people were staring. Carter sat by himself a few tables away. He lifted his soda in Bryce's direction and gave a small smile.

"So, you can walk, first of all," Gabby said, gesturing to Bryce's legs. "How is that possible?"

"Gab, let her off the hook for a second." Greg addressed Gabby, but he couldn't take his eyes off Bryce. She bit her lip, looking down when she met his intense, deep-blue gaze. "She just sat down."

"No, it's all right," Bryce said. "I've had to work my ass off," she began, and at the sight of them sitting there, waiting, everything poured out of her. She told them about waking up, about the hospital, about Carter and Dr. Warren. They listened, commenting and laughing at all the right moments. They waved away the waitress. They asked questions.

As she finished telling them about Sydney, her parents, and the weird new house, Bryce's eyes filled with tears. "I'm not sad," Bryce said, and it was true. "It's just so nice you're finally here."

Gabby chirped, "We could say the same for you!"

Greg just looked at Bryce through his long lashes.

Bryce wiped her eyes on a paper napkin. It was a little embarrassing. She shifted. "So what's up with you guys?"

Gabby glanced at Greg quickly, as if choosing who should go first. Seeming to make up her mind, Gabby dove in. "I'm going to be a lawyer," she said firmly.

Gabby flowed and fluttered through what she had done, how much fun college had been, and then wove slowly into the sad parts: quitting diving to focus on academics, missing home and Nashville. She was headed to GW Law in the fall.

"And Greg," she began. Greg had been interjecting *yes*es

and *nos*, but said nothing of what he had done. He just sat leaning back, smiling or shrugging at Bryce when Gabby said ridiculous things. Like always. "Greg's also going to be in D.C. Finding a job."

"Really?"

"I don't know," Greg said, fumbling. He seemed surprised, as if he had been thinking about something else. "I like D.C. a lot. Pretty buildings."

Bryce raised her eyebrows, trying to picture Greg in the capital, wearing a suit maybe, doing a desk job. He'd always had ideas for eclectic businesses, like selling boat radar detectors or organic horse feed, a new one every week. But maybe that was just the kind of thing you talked about in high school. "People go through phases," her father had warned her after she'd hung up the phone last night. Bryce wouldn't know. She hadn't had the chance to grow out of anything.

"What about coaching, though?" she asked Greg intently. "Did you give up diving, too?"

"No, no." Greg smiled back, his full lips breaking cheeks into dimples. "I rode it out. But not all of us have the whistle-blowing skills of Mike Graham."

Gabby smiled at him, wrinkling her nose, then turned to Bryce. "So, what's next for you?"

"I don't know. Want to watch a movie?" Bryce smiled

hopefully. She had been looking forward to doing that, just the three of them. Just hanging out, like old times. Maybe they could come over after this. They could watch a Western, maybe some John Wayne, like *The Searchers.* Gabby would yield now, Bryce knew she would. Or maybe she would get her way as always and make them watch *Pride and Prejudice,* coma or no coma, arguing that Bryce hadn't seen it in five years.

Gabby cracked up. "No, I mean, like, your life."

Bryce opened her mouth to answer, then closed it. Her life had been all planned out—the Olympics, diving for Vanderbilt, another Olympics. After that, maybe she'd coach, or if she was lucky, keep training, keep diving, keep competing. Now she didn't know. Her family, diving, and Greg were the only things she'd ever loved. The only things she'd ever really known at all.

"Not much of anything yet," she said.

"We'll find something," Gabby said knowingly. "You've missed a lot, but there's still time to figure it out."

Bryce felt a strange twinge in her gut that she wasn't used to feeling around them. Greg and Gabby knew who they were and what they wanted. Bryce should be happy for them, she knew that. But she didn't feel happy. She felt like she needed to defend herself for being asleep for five years.

As Greg took the last chip, the hostess came by. "Are you sure y'all don't want anything to drink?"

"Oh, I can't—" Bryce began, then she stopped. This wouldn't be like that time in Bryan Godard's basement when she and Gabby were dared to drink vodka straight out of the bottle. They were adults now, right? "You know what? I'll take one."

"So, three margaritas?" Gabby said, raising her eyebrows at Bryce

"Yep." Bryce nodded. She looked at the hostess. "You need ID?"

"Ha. Yeah, right," the hostess replied shortly, and walked away.

"Oooh, Bry's famous," Gabby teased.

Bryce blushed and looked at Greg, wearing the same old Hanes T-shirt out of a five-pack, twisting two straws together with his long, bitten-down fingertips. He was different, but he was still the same old Greg, mostly. He used to ride home with Bryce after practice on weekends and raid the refrigerator. He talked technique with her dad, fixing an odd shelf or curtain rod for her mother while Sydney followed him around, asking unnecessary questions. She used to joke that he was better at being a Graham than she was.

"So," Bryce said. She looked back and forth between the

two of them, as if they were all lounging on the bleachers after a meet.

"So," Gabby replied. But then her brow started to wrinkle, and her eyes squinted, holding back tears. "Oh, Bryce. We never thought we'd see you again."

Another lump formed in Bryce's throat. "It must have been hard."

"It was." Gabby nodded and let her eyes drift toward Greg. She spun her ring around her finger nervously. "The only thing that made it okay was that we had each other."

Greg returned Gabby's gaze, long enough for Bryce to feel like she had disappeared, just for a moment. She frowned. *We had each other.* It sounded odd, like something one of the characters from Gabby's romance novels would say.

Gabby continued quietly. "The reason why I asked you what was next for you is because we want to share something that's next for us."

Gabby kept looking at Greg. Why was she looking at Greg so much? Greg looked back at Gabby, and then at the floor. He looked sad. Tense. Nervous.

"What?" Bryce asked. What did she mean, *us*?

"Do you remember how you thought Redding Greenberg had cooties when you were in third grade?"

Bryce laughed. "Yeah, of course."

"And then, one day, you woke up and you felt so differently. You wrote his name in little hearts, and chased him on the playground." Bryce felt herself turning red, but Gabby pressed on. "You did. You know you did."

"I did," Bryce admitted, smiling. "And?" she said, sipping water.

"Try to imagine that happening . . . but, like, now."

Greg finally looked up. "Really, Gab? That's how you're going to do this?"

Bryce looked back and forth between them, trying and failing to meet their eyes. Her mind was blank, but her muscles began to tighten with fear.

Gabby continued, her voice trembling. "Like all of a sudden, you wake up, and things are different. You love someone who's been there all along. And it's so random, but that's just the way you feel." Gabby looked vulnerable now, like she was about to shatter.

"Greg and I," Gabby went on, her voice getting smaller. "I . . . we've been together, Bryce. We're actually, um. We're engaged," she said, and then she said some more, but Bryce didn't hear the rest. After the word *engaged*, the dinner rush at Los Pollitos filled her ears. The hum of the lights, the clanking of silverware, the conversation next to them.

The noise rose to a deafening roar, but no one else seemed

to hear it. Hot pain crept from her neck, pricking her forehead, her eyes.

"I just need to—" Bryce began, snapping her eyes shut to the hurt that was beginning to shoot from her spine. She couldn't finish. She fell backward, or forward, she couldn't tell, and opened her eyes to a strange sight.

The barn.

Nighttime had fallen, making the walls and ceiling almost disappear. But this was a special place. Bryce knew exactly where the beams stood, where the stalls were, where the floor creaked. She didn't need to see. And suddenly, a light came on, forming a small circle near the hayloft.

Bryce looked up. A halo of blond hair, the angles of a muscled shoulder. Greg.

Greg set the electric lantern on the floor of the barn, the light illuminating his face in sharp shadows. His lips pressed together, shaking. He looked like he had hurt himself. He was crying. Then he said her name.

Bryce took a step toward him, only to trip on nothing through nothingness, landing back on a chair, blinking rapidly, out of breath.

Gabby was looking at her with the same wincing expression. Bryce clutched the table, suddenly afraid it was going to tip from under her.

"Engaged to be married?" Bryce finally asked. She tried to swallow. There was a hot rock wedged in her throat.

The waitress brought their margaritas, and Gabby took a small, tentative sip. Greg gulped his down. Bryce watched the lime-green liquid of the drink get lower and lower until it was gone.

"Greg asked me when we were in Italy. I know that's not—I can't even imagine . . . I wish there was some other . . . I know this must be weird," Gabby finally finished. She absently spun her ring around her finger again, and for the first time, Bryce really looked at it. It was a gold ring with a small yellow diamond, and it sat on the ring finger of her left hand. An engagement ring. Of course it was an engagement ring. Bryce hadn't given it a second thought. People wore class rings, rings given to them from their grandparents. Nobody got *married*. Not *them*.

Greg's hand rested beside his glass. Gabby took it. Bryce felt like something was snaking out of her gut. Her intestines maybe.

"Just say whatever you feel," Gabby said.

"I don't—have anything," Bryce croaked. The hot rock was making it hard to speak.

Greg let go of Gabby's hand. Bryce felt no relief.

"In a way, it's a blessing," Gabby said. "The timing—I *knew* we were right to come back to Nashville for the wedding. It would mean so much to us if you would be there."

"Be there?" Bryce choked out.

Gabby sputtered, shaking her head. "Well, if you felt like it was something you could do. I mean, I have no idea. All I can say is . . ." She took a shuddery breath. "We didn't know, Bryce. We didn't know," she repeated. "I'm just so glad you came back to us."

Bryce would not look at Greg. She felt him sitting there, now ripping apart his napkin. She took a sip of margarita, and her mouth twisted at its salty-sweet bitterness.

Gabby's face gradually broke into a small smile. "I just . . . Growing up, I always pictured you next to me at my wedding. I couldn't imagine who the groom would be. It didn't matter. I just knew you'd be my maid of honor." She leaned forward anxiously under the hanging lamp. She was wearing makeup. Mascara that brought her lashes to a long, vicious swoop. Blush the color of sunset, at the tip of her cheekbones. "Will you? Be my maid of honor?"

Gabby stared at her. But then she looked up, past Bryce. Bryce felt a warm hand on her shoulder and turned around.

"Sorry to be a downer, but you're not in stable enough

condition to drink alcohol." Carter spoke directly to her, not looking across the table. "Also, I just got a call from your parents. They need you at home."

"Oh." Gabby sat up straighter, looking at Carter with concern. "Are you her nurse?"

Carter let out a snort. "Kind of."

Bryce couldn't help but untwist her mouth into a small smile. Relief swept through her. It felt good to be needed somewhere. She limped away with Carter at her side, the ground like liquid beneath her feet.

"Bryce!" she heard Gabby call.

She turned to look at the couple, now blurred across the restaurant.

"Talk to you soon, okay?" Gabby's voice sounded tentative.

Bryce finally looked at Greg, but it was as if the moment her gaze met his, he shrank away, disappearing. She turned and walked away from them, pushing open the doors harder than she needed to.

CHAPTER SEVEN

Though it was nearly evening, the parking lot was still bathed in bright light, the low sun beating off the car hoods and windows. Bryce supported herself on the parked cars, surrounded by the sounds of distant traffic and the dull thump of her boots on the asphalt. The cicadas buzzed.

Carter came a few feet behind her, and they arrived at his car.

"What happened?" Bryce said softly, trying to match the quiet. "Is it Sydney? Is everything okay?"

Carter leaned against the Honda. "I made that up. Your parents didn't call."

Bryce blew out the breath she'd been holding. "Ah, okay."

"I thought I heard you guys ordering drinks so I started listening in. It didn't sound good."

Bryce said nothing. Maybe she should be angry with Carter for sticking his nose in her business, but after the news she'd just heard, it seemed like a small offense.

"I thought you'd want out of there."

"Too much excitement for my rusty ol' brain. Good work, doctor." She started to take short, pained steps past the car.

"Where are you going?"

"I don't know," she replied. "I just need to move." As she said this, she realized how stupid she sounded, as if getting her body away from what had just happened would keep it away for good. She used to do the same thing as a little kid. A plate broke, she fell down and skinned her knee, she would just scramble away as if bad things only happened in one place. She turned, leaning against the warm metal of the car.

Carter opened the driver's door. "You want to go home?"

"Yep," she said, although she'd been awake for long enough now to know that home didn't exist anymore.

＊

The seats were warm and the windows were down. Bryce held out her hand to catch drops of water from the sprinklers. Carter had started to tell her about a book he'd been reading.

The sound of his voice was oddly soothing, the up and down, but all Bryce could do was look out at the houses whizzing by, letting the water droplets hit her arm. If Bryce focused hard enough, she could see each individual droplet catch the gold light as it flew through the air and then follow its arc over the sidewalks, over the curb, shattering against her skin as if it were made of glass.

Beautiful, Bryce thought. She wished Carter could see what she was seeing.

They pulled up in front of the big blue house. The restaurant, Gabby and Greg engaged, it was all catching up. She couldn't act like she was happy for them, like they were two people she knew from long ago, like an old high school friend would act. They didn't feel like people from her past. One day she'd fallen asleep, and the next her boyfriend was engaged to her best friend.

Diving, the van trips to tournaments, Gabby insisting they play gin rummy, lying in the bed of Greg's pickup truck, dancing with Greg in the barn with no music . . . it was all last month to her.

It didn't matter that they were getting married. Walking down the aisle, wearing nice clothes, that was a game. It was that they were in love, that they probably needed each other, relied on each other. They kissed each other. My god, they probably had sex. And it meant something. Her stomach twisted painfully. It probably meant everything. Which left her with what? Nothing.

Bryce could disappear into a coma again and their lives would go on as planned.

She had been flailing above the truth like she was treading water, and now she let go. Bryce slumped in her seat.

Carter took off his seat belt. "You okay?" he asked.

She looked at him, and tears came. She tried to swallow them. "They're engaged," she said.

"I know," he said solemnly.

Bryce remembered her dad's warning about phases. Her mom trying desperately to get her to stay home. Sydney that first night at the hospital. Bryce was the only one in the dark. They had all left her in the dark. Or maybe she had put herself there on purpose. She didn't know which was worse.

"How could they do that?"

Carter tightened his lips and shook his head. "I don't know." He moved his hand to Bryce's shoulder, letting it rest there for a second, leaving a trail of warmth on Bryce's skin.

Bryce sniffed, shuddering, and lifted her boots to rest them on the dashboard. She was still restrained by her seat belt.

Carter reached over. "Here," he said, and clicked the buckle open. The seat belt slid back into place. "I normally don't let people put their feet on the dash, but I guess we can make an exception."

"Gee, thanks," Bryce said.

Carter sighed, and shut off the engine. "The time passing probably hits harder sometimes than at others."

"You think?" Bryce had a sudden urge to slap Carter in the face. Not because he had done anything, but because he was there, facing her like Greg had faced her that day at the lake. She wanted to go back to that day so badly now. She would swim away from Greg, and she would walk past Gabby under the tree. She would live the next five years of her life without them, as they had done without her.

"You'll get through all of this," Carter said. "You're strong." He was rubbing his chin again, thinking. His eyes darted from her boots on the dashboard to her face, back to the boots.

"I hope so," Bryce said.

"No, you will," Carter said. He spoke more gently now, evenly, like someone who would know because it was his job to make it that way. "Really."

They sat there, listening to her take choppy breaths. She let tears fall on her lap, closing her eyes. She didn't care about crying in front of Carter anymore. At that moment, she didn't care about much of anything.

Through the dark red of her eyelids, Bryce felt Carter reach out to her, and that was how she met him in the center of the two seats, her head burrowing easily into a place in his chest, his arms fitting around her.

It was nice. She hadn't been hugged like that in a long time. Nowadays people squeezed her quickly, just for a second, as if they might break her. This is nice, she thought again.

Carter loosened, Bryce leaned back, and somehow her forehead was right near his chin.

Oops, Bryce thought. She tilted her head to say sorry. But she didn't end up saying sorry.

Her mouth had found its way to his. His lips were soft, but Bryce could feel pressure behind them. They moved again, to fit hers.

After a moment, Bryce pulled away. "Whoa," she said quietly.

"Bryce . . ."

"Um, I should . . ." She opened the door without finishing her sentence. She kept her eyes down and stepped out onto the pavement.

"Bryce," Carter called through the open door, but she shut it behind her before he could say more. Her heartbeat pulsed in her fingertips. She stepped slowly up the walkway and around the side of the house. She looked back as Carter finally pulled away. Night was coming, and fireflies started making dots in the tall plants lining the curb.

If a day like this happened five years ago, she would have immediately called her best friend. She would have said hi to her parents sitting in the living room, with her phone already to her ear, gone down to her room, flopped on her bed with a handful of trail mix, and figured things out.

But she couldn't do any of that. Her room wasn't her room, her best friend wasn't waiting at home for her call.

Bryce stayed in the middle of the lawn, surrounded by the stretching road and scattered houses, and realized River Drive was the only thing that hadn't changed.

It was the people—the people settling into their houses, those people and the thick pastures that separated them, the GO TENNESSEE! signs on their long lawns—it was them Bryce had to ask:

"What the hell?"

Nobody answered, of course, and she went inside.

CHAPTER EIGHT

Bryce found her mother in her home office at the back of the house, her face glowing blue from the monitor's light. The office used to be the place where Bryce and Sydney kicked off their muddy galoshes or threw their coats, but now the small space was outfitted with a flat-screen computer and prints of some of the spaces her mother had designed. Out of habit, or maybe because she refused to acknowledge this wasn't the mudroom anymore, Bryce kicked off her boots and set them in the corner. Her mother turned to face her.

"You knew," Bryce said accusingly.

Her mom sat up in her Aeron chair, her spine stiff. "About Greg and Gabby? Are they . . . ?" She slumped. "I had heard they were dating," she admitted.

"Engaged," Bryce said, making her hands into fists. The sky outside the tall windows had faded to black. "Not dating. Engaged." She tried to make her words hard. She wanted to hold on to the anger, to feel anything besides emptiness. But the anger was slipping away from her, out of her grasp, like water down a drain. Her lip began to quiver.

"No," her mom whispered, getting up from the desk to put an arm around Bryce. "Oh, honey."

At first Bryce tried to resist, but then she let her head fall on her mother's shoulder. She used to do the same thing when she had done badly at meets, when her father's face fell in disappointment. She felt that way now. Like she had lost.

Her mother's voice sounded quiet above her. "I had hoped it was just a college thing. I didn't want to say anything in case they weren't still together, but . . ." With her head in the crook of her shoulder, Bryce could feel her mother shake her head. "I should have told you. It was stupid of me. I should have told you."

She let her mother rock her back and forth, closing her eyes.

"It's okay, Mom," Bryce said, even though it wasn't. It

might never be okay again, but right now that seemed somehow beside the point.

*

"At least the toilet is clean," Bryce called through the crack in the door. It was the next day, and she was standing outside the only indoor restroom of the Belle Meade mansion.

"The toilet *was* clean," Sydney's voice corrected, and Bryce heard the sounds of retching.

Bryce tried not to feel nauseous herself. The potpourri and decrepit lace that covered every surface of the old Southern house didn't help.

"Girls?" their mother called from down the hall. "Everything okay?"

Bryce slipped into the bathroom, holding her nose. "Mom's coming," she said, panicky. Sydney shrugged from her kneeling position on the cracked tile.

"Yep, Sydney's just having stomach issues," Bryce called, peeking from behind the door. "Must have been bad cream cheese."

"Don't even bother," Sydney said, still halfway inside the bowl. "They know I'm hungover."

"I'm just trying to help," Bryce said.

"Don't," Sydney replied shortly. "You can leave now."

Bryce sighed. That morning, her mom had helped her

upstairs to see her dad and Sydney gathered in the kitchen, Sydney's eye makeup running from the night before.

"Family outing," Sydney had muttered, and they piled into the van.

Her face had become increasingly pale on the winding drive to the other edge of Nashville. Their mother chattered up front about how they used to go to Belle Meade when the girls were small.

"Y'all just loved the horses," her mom had said, adopting the accent of the reenactors who wandered the historical plantation in Civil War–era clothes.

Sydney had put her arms inside her oversized Ramones T-shirt and swallowed what was probably puke.

Now she stood up from the toilet, wiping her mouth. Her face was still tinged green.

"You look like a kid on one of those Just Say No posters," Bryce said.

"You would know all about being a poster child, wouldn't you?" Sydney responded, scrunching her brunette curls in the mirror.

Bryce stood beside Sydney. They were the same height and had the same hazel eyes. Their dad's eyes. Dad's dark eyebrows. Their mother's ski-jump nose. If Bryce pushed back her waves, the blond disappearing, they nearly looked like twins. Minus the lip-piercing and heavy eyeliner. Bryce wondered vaguely what Sydney would look like now if she had been around.

"What is it like to be hungover?" she asked Sydney's pale reflection.

Sydney made a face and turned to her sister. "I don't know, Bryce. What is it like to wake up from a coma?"

"Touché," Bryce said.

Their mother was waiting around the corner of the creaky mansion corridor with a new piece of plantation trivia, a small shopping bag hanging from her wrist. Their father looked comically out of place near the grand staircase, staring up at portraits in his Vanderbilt T-shirt and athletic shorts.

"You remember this one, Bryce?"

He pointed to an intricate portrait of a woman in a blue hoop skirt, her fan poised as it would be on a sweltering day like today. Her hair was slicked and her rouge formed perfect small circles, but she had a sparkle in her eye like she had just done something she shouldn't.

"The Southern Mona Lisa." Bryce smiled.

Her mother let out a happy sigh and wrapped Bryce in a hug.

Sydney twisted her curls into a messy bun and grabbed

her phone from a nearby table. "I'm going back out to the car," she announced.

Bryce's father looked at Sydney, his lips in a straight line. "We just got here."

Her mother shot her dad a look. "Are you sure, sweetie?" she said awkwardly, her arm around Bryce. "You want some pop or something?"

"Nah, you don't need me now that the prodigal daughter has returned." Sydney gestured to Bryce.

"Come on, Syd. Don't be like that," Bryce said.

"Screw off, Bryce," Sydney said with a fake smile, and she turned to the door.

✻

They decided to call it a day when her mom stepped in a pile of droppings left by the geese that roamed the front lawn. Though her dad laughed a little too heartily, he bent over with an old newspaper to wipe off his wife's loafers. When Bryce saw Sydney again, she was leaning against the white-washed fence, staring at the horses as she massaged her head.

The sycamores seemed oddly still to Bryce without the constant chirp of cicadas, but they didn't come out until sunset. Her father used to wager he could hear them even in the daytime, if everyone held their breath for a long time, as quiet as they could be. Bryce could never really be sure if she could actually hear them, or if it was just that she wanted to believe him.

She stepped lightly underneath the mossy branches, only hobbling slightly, her legs sore from the constant effort. Dr. Warren said her body would never be at its best again, but what did she know? Bryce fanned herself against the wet heat.

And then she heard it, brief but clear: the high, chirping cry of a cicada. At first it echoed like it came from far away, and then it seemed to push through the silence and join with another call right next to her, as full and clear as if it were beside her ear. Bryce moved a hand up to touch it, but nothing was there. I knew that, she mused. They're far away. I can tell. She put her hand down. They're waiting for night. The calls came again, washing over her, making the air around her pulse.

After a moment, it stopped. The midday sun broke through in patches, and the trees were silent once more.

She set the fan down at her side and turned her face up to the sky. She was here on Earth, wasn't she? She was better off than she was a month ago. She looked down at her feet, so pale in strappy sandals against the green grass. She needed sun. She needed exercise. It was time to accept that things were different, but she could be different, too.

"Bryce, honey!" her mother called to her from where their van was parked. "Let's go!"

She looked at her family, her mother next to the SUV, her father at the steering wheel, and Sydney, her long legs stretched across the bucket seat, closing the door. They may not be as happy as they used to be, but they were there, together, and Bryce was awake, alive, walking toward them.

✳

Back on River Drive, Bryce stepped down the stairs and let out an "Ahhh" at the air-conditioning. She moved slowly across the basement tile in her bare feet and stripped off her damp tank top and shorts, tossing them in the hamper in the corner of her room. She opened her closet. Nothing but everyone's old clothes and a pair of skis.

Clothes, she added to the list. Sun, exercise, and clothes. She chose an old tunic of her mother's from the seventies. Nothing fancy, Bryce thought as she pulled the white cotton over her head. Literally, just clothes of my own. The tunic was short on her but it would have to do.

"Bryce!" her father called down the stairs. Bryce groaned. Her name sounded loud and short when her father yelled it, as if he were yelling "Go!" at diving practice.

"What?" Bryce yelled back.

"Carter is here!"

Carter. She sat on her bed. Oh god, oh god, oh god, Bryce thought.

"He's just gonna come around back," her father yelled.

"No!" Bryce yelled.

"What?" her father yelled.

"Never mind," Bryce said. It was pointless, she saw as she came out of her room and spotted Carter through the glass doors, making his way down the hill. He stopped at the pool, staring down into the water. Her father had cleaned it recently, and it was back to its pristine turquoise blue.

Bryce took a deep breath. What should she say? "Why?" was the only thing she could think of.

Carter had picked a leaf and was crouched over the pool with it, trying to help a floating bug to safety. Bryce jiggled her arms a little bit to relax, like she used to do on the platform before she dove. She swallowed and walked through the doors onto the patio.

"Hi," Carter said, looking at a spot above her head.

Bryce could see that he had just come from the hospital. He was still wearing his ID badge on the pocket of a worn button-down shirt, through which she could see the lines of his upper half. He was lean and long and solid, all the way from his broad shoulders down to the waist of his khaki cutoffs.

"Hey," Bryce said, trying not to smile.

"How are you feeling?"

"Great," Bryce responded. He was now staring at his feet. Bryce continued, "I mean, physically. I'm sore, but . . . good."

"Good," he echoed.

"Yeah," Bryce said, looking at him pointedly. He still avoided her eyes. Was he going to say something about the other day? She wished he would make a joke. This clean, formal version of Carter was making her nervous. "Am I due to go in for a checkup or something?"

"Kind of," he said. "Remember when you made me take you to that restaurant?"

Before Bryce could nod, he continued. "I forgot to tell you. Before I left, I told Dr. Warren where I was going. She said it was a good idea. Didn't seem to think you'd be coming in much on your own. So. She decided to work something out where you don't have to go all the way to the medical center, if you don't want to."

"I don't want to," Bryce said quickly. "I definitely do not want to."

"There ya go," Carter said, shrugging.

"And instead . . ."

"I will be checking up. On you," he said slowly, almost one word at a time.

"Is that standard procedure?" she asked, tilting her head, smiling.

He squinted off into the distance. "Not really."

Bryce made her way over to the edge of the pool, where Carter's bug was crawling away. "You know, if med school doesn't work out, you could always find work rescuing drowning insects."

Finally, a small laugh. "At least then I wouldn't be tempted by beautiful patients."

Bryce froze, looking at him.

"What happened the other day was completely out of line. I apologize."

"That's okay," Bryce said, but cursed herself immediately afterward. She should say something more—well, more official. But she was distracted. Carter had said she was beautiful. He had just gone ahead and said it. "Apology accepted," she added.

"And it wasn't professional," Carter went on, taking a breath. "Not only was it unprofessional, it was inappropriate. You know, to what—to what you were feeling at the time."

"Right," Bryce said. But she didn't mean "right."

She looked at him. His brow was unfurrowed, but his head was still down. "So." He looked up at her and forced a smile. "Do you remember what 'checking vital signs' means?"

Bryce smiled back. "Is that what they call it these days?"

Carter blushed. "It means you'll have to stay in one place for ten minutes. Can you do that?"

"I can try," Bryce said with mock exasperation, and sat gingerly on a pool chair while Carter removed a stethoscope from his shoulder bag.

He kneeled next to her and put the cold disc to her chest. Bryce felt an electric jolt with his hand near her skin. He stared in concentration, his mouth turned down at the corners.

"A little fast, but consistent," he said after a minute, looking at his watch.

He recorded the number on her chart. Bryce could see somebody had typed her name incorrectly on the top of the paper; BRICE GRAHAM, it read. Carter had crossed out the *i* and replaced it with a *y* in his own scratchy writing. He took her blood pressure and temperature, staying quiet all the while.

"Well." He stood up.

For some reason the motion was too fast for Bryce.

A small fire seemed to travel up the base of her neck, to her skull, behind her eyes. At first, Bryce just thought she was blushing, but no, this was a real fire. Pain branded the top of her spine and traveled in shots of heat to her forehead. *This again.* She looked down, trying to get control.

"Wait," she tried to say.

But the cement by the pool turned on its side. Again, she fell. It was almost as if Bryce moved forward right into it, like a wall.

A spring day.

She was looking through a crack in the hospital curtain. A young man in a white shirt was facing away from her, bending over a bed. There lay Bryce's body in a light-blue gown.

The young man pulled the covers closer to her face as a cool breeze came through the open window, washing away the hospital smell. He sat down on one of the empty chairs and cracked open a book with a gold cover and a deep red spine.

The sound was clear. No crackling or buzzing, just the sweet song of birds from outside. He began to speak.

"I, uh. I heard you like Westerns." He cleared his throat. "This is a biography of Wyatt Earp. Ahem. Sheriff Wyatt Earp was a man of swift and decisive action. . . ."

The poolside cement appeared again, like it was knocking her over, and she was tipped back to the chair. Her head jerked back.

The hot pain flashed once again, then faded into cool relief. She blinked, situated herself, and shook her hands out of the numb feeling.

"Yeah? Do you need something?" Carter was saying, standing over her. "Bryce?"

Bryce shook the vision away. "Huh?" she said, pulling her mother's tunic around her legs. She bit her lip. "No."

"All right, then," he said, putting his bag over his shoulder. "Stay healthy." He looked at Bryce. "I mean that." He turned away from her, heading up the hill.

"Carter, wait." Bryce blinked slowly.

Flashes of what she had just seen would not leave her. The person by the bed. The way his voice sounded. There was something connecting them to the reality of Carter next to her, right then. Something had just fallen into place.

Carter stopped.

"You spent a lot of time with me when I was asleep, didn't you?" she asked. "You were there."

Carter found Bryce's eyes and held them there for a second. A long second, puzzling. "Almost every day."

And with that, Carter continued up the hill. Bryce watched his figure as he disappeared around the house. He was a person from her strange dreams, but she didn't know him before her accident. She had known he was with her while she slept—before anyone told her.

Which meant that the visions from her bedside were not just visions. They were real.

Bryce leaned against the chair, her stomach in knots. Gray clouds were collecting over the sun, fading the blue sky like a sheet washed too many times. Little laps of the now darkening pool water spilled over the sides—the wind had picked up this afternoon.

She closed her eyes, trying to bring up the scenes like the one she had just been inside of. Tipping back and forth from her hospital room, her body behind the blue curtain; Sydney as a child; her parents drifting around her like they barely knew each other; Greg in the barn; Carter sitting, reading on a spring day she had never known. They were all looped in her mind now, somehow.

Something had gone too far when her brain reignited. She could be in a time where she wasn't supposed to be, she could see what she wasn't supposed to see. Colors seemed to fall on her like overturned buckets of paint, and each sound was its own little orchestra. Her senses were wide open now, and they would stay that way, wider than she could have ever imagined.

As heavy drops began to fall, Bryce couldn't help but raise her hand to her head. She almost expected it to shock her. But it felt just like it always had.

"Bryce, get inside!" Her mother called from the sliding door. "There's going to be lightning."

Carter knew that I liked Westerns. She would see him again soon, and again the day after that. At the thought of that, she smiled.

Sun, exercise, clothes. Bryce went over her list again as she reentered through the French doors. *And friends.*

The emptiness she'd felt wasn't emptiness anymore. It was space to be filled.

CHAPTER NINE

The air wrapped Bryce in a blanket of moisture. The leaves on the oak tree in the Grahams' front yard stood still, waxy and green. There was no breeze. The lawn was thriving like a football field, so bright it almost looked fake. Bryce wished she could suck up water from the humidity like the plants could. She had stepped outside to wait for Gabby five minutes ago, and she could already use a tall glass of something.

After Carter walked away yesterday, Bryce had felt powerful. She had felt full of good things. *Only good things,* she had declared, and she had gone straight inside to call

Gabby, eager to tell her that everything was going to be okay. Gabby picked up on the first ring. "Bryce."

Bryce's confidence had faltered at the sound of her voice. It was easy enough to forgive her best friend when she was thinking of the Gabby whose perfect fishtail braid she used to mess up, the one who she could tease about being a hopeless romantic because she was too wrapped up in a soap opera plot to notice.

But this wasn't quite Gabby. Her voice had an edge now.

"So what's the deal with the bridesmaid thing?" Bryce had asked.

"Oh," Gabby said, and Bryce could hear the surprise in her voice. "So you don't want to talk—?"

She had looked at the storm outside, thinking again of Carter as he walked away. She swallowed her fear.

"Let's meet up!" Bryce said, before Gabby could say anything else. "If I'm going to be your maid of honor, I'm going to need a dress, right?"

They agreed Gabby would pick her up for a trip to the mall. "Just to start," Gabby had said. "Because you also need regular clothes."

"How did you know?" Bryce said.

"Believe me, I recognized your mom's old pajama top." Bryce had to smile.

A black VW pulled up. Different from the van Gabby

usually drove. Used to drive, Bryce corrected herself. But then Gabby honked twice, like she always did, and Bryce made her way down the walk.

"Hi, gorgeous!" Gabby called as she leaned to open the door. The air-conditioning was blasting. Gabby's lavender shampoo filled Bryce's nose, and suddenly they were sixteen again, driving to practice, to a football game, anywhere. "How are you?"

"Went to Belle Meade yesterday," Bryce started. "Sydney was hungover, as usual."

"Oh god." Gabby glanced from the road. "Sydney's one of *those* girls?"

Bryce knew exactly what she meant—the girls at their school who mixed vodka into gas-station slushies at football games, who partied every weekend while she and Gabby trained or went to meets.

Bryce shook her head. "I mean, she wouldn't be part of, like, Renee Sutterlane's clique. She's a little too punk-goth-whatever for that. Those girls always pretended to be Christian."

"And they all got pregnant, like, right out of high school," Gabby said, shaking her head.

"What? Really?"

"Renee has two kids now. Kat O'Hare has a baby with Chris Driggs. Kylie Timmons has one with who knows who."

Bryce laughed in disbelief. "Wow. That *sucks*." She could barely take care of herself, let alone a baby.

"I don't know, Bry." Gabby looked thoughtful. "They look really happy on Facebook. They dress their babies in these cute little outfits. . . ."

"Gabbyyyyy—" Bryce chided. "Don't get any ideas."

Gabby pursed her glossy lips. "Come on, wouldn't it be fun to have an adorable little baby?"

"No!" Bryce shook her finger at her friend. "Just say no!"

"Fine," Gabby said, her lips still pursed, but then she smiled.

Bryce smiled into the rearview mirror, watching suburbia shrink as they got closer to downtown Nashville.

Gabby sighed as they pulled up to a red light. "Besides, Greg is *not* ready to be a father."

Bryce's chest tightened. She had been lulled by the comfort of Gabby's familiar smell, the feeling of sitting in the passenger seat. For just a moment, she had forgotten.

Gabby glanced at her. "I tried to get him to come with us today, maybe try on some tuxedoes, but he said, 'Nah.' That's exactly what he said. 'Nah.'"

Bryce's jaw clenched. The cars around them started to move. This was the part they should glaze over. This was the part that would make her pissed off. But they were going dress-shopping, and he was the groom. Did she think she could avoid it forever?

They jerked forward. Silence. Greg's name was ringing in Bryce's ears.

Finally, Gabby broke the silence. Her voice was grave. "Bryce, I have something to tell you."

Bryce's stomach was in knots. What now?

Gabby opened her mouth, but instead of speaking, she hit the CD player's ON button. A few chords filtered out, and Bryce recognized the song instantly.

"Yeah, B. Talk your shit," Gabby said in her best Jay-Z impression.

Bryce always played the Beyoncé part, because then Gabby could call her "B." She let out a throaty, "Partner, let me upgrade you," and immediately giggled with embarrassment. Like most things these days, Bryce was out of practice singing like an R&B star.

As they pulled into the mall parking lot, Bryce and Gabby danced Beyoncé-style in their seats, swinging their hips and flipping their hair. "Upgrade U" was the first track on their warm-up CD. This was what they pumped from Bryce's basement speakers as they practiced tucks at her house. This was what they sang to as they rolled into Hilwood High in the mornings. The CD even skipped at the right place.

Bryce yelled over the Jay-Z part, "Where did you find this?"

"Are you kidding?" Gabby yelled back between lines. "I would never have let this thing out of my sight!"

As she nodded her head to the beat, Bryce dabbed sudden, grateful tears with the back of her hand. She smiled at her best friend. A thank-you for this little part of Bryce's old life, and for letting the subject of Greg drop. They kept rapping and dancing as they entered the mall, doubling over with laughter at the shoppers who stared as they passed.

✳

An hour later, everything was chiffon. Layers of the light-pink, netlike fabric surrounded Bryce. She climbed through them, the edges of each piece tickling her face. Suddenly she was in the open air again, staring at her own reflection. The dress was very puffy and very pink.

"I look like one of those shower pouf things."

"Let me see," Gabby said, and pushed her way into the dressing room. She caught Bryce's eyes in the mirror, and there was an awkward pause. There had been a lot of those since Bryce had filled up her Macy's bags with T-shirts and Gabby pulled an issue of *Modern Bride* out of her purse. She had asked if Bryce wanted to take a break while they looked through it, maybe get some Orange Julius. She even offered to take Bryce home to rest, but Bryce was determined not to let the mood fall, not when things were starting to feel normal between them.

"I just thought it would be interesting." Gabby twisted a strand of her hair around her finger, looking worried. "You know, different from the average bridesmaid dress."

"No, it's nice," Bryce said. The top of the dress was pretty. Kind of soft, not too shiny, with a cut right at her bust line. But then it exploded. "Different is good."

"But not always good," Gabby offered quickly. "Here, let's get it off. Now we've narrowed it down. We need something more classic. Maybe slimmer lines."

She stepped out of the dressing room while Bryce wriggled out through the forest of chiffon.

"See, my . . . er, dress is really traditional," Gabby said in the eveningwear section when Bryce emerged, moving through different shades of red. "I was thinking bigger shapes, something more elaborate to provide a contrast."

Gabby picked out a long, silky dress in vivid red. She pulled Bryce into an oversized dressing room with an upholstered chair in the corner. "But now that I think of it, maybe consistency would work better. Here." She laid the dress out on Bryce's open arms.

Gabby took a seat, looking at her, but Bryce didn't move to change immediately. She had changed in front of Gabby a thousand times, but Bryce found herself setting the dress aside slowly and bringing her arms inside her T-shirt before she slid it above her navel, her eyes avoiding Gabby's.

"Oh," Gabby said, realizing, and busied herself with her purse.

Bryce had always been modest, waiting to take off her warm-up until immediately before she dove, refusing to be interviewed post-dive until she had put it back on. But ever since her body had failed her, it felt foreign to her. She understood her limbs and back and stomach as a diver's, as an athlete's who used every muscle for a certain purpose. When other girls were getting curves, Bryce and Gabby were "manly" together, as Gabby had called it. Built to be slick, aerodynamic, but not really, well, *feminine*.

Now neither of them were athletes. Their muscles lay dormant, covered by curves. *Why here?* Bryce had found herself asking of her newly thickened thighs when she squeezed into Sydney's jeans, or earlier that day, when she had spilled out of a B cup.

Bryce stepped into the red dress, looking at Gabby's turned back with a pang of guilt. *I've been avoiding mirrors,* Bryce wanted to tell her, but she knew that would sound weird.

Even now, as she stood in the center of her threefold reflection, Bryce blurred her eyes until she was just a long blob of red. "Okay!" she tried to say with enthusiasm. *"Voilà."*

Gabby looked up and gasped. "Bryce," she said, putting her hands up to her mouth. "You're stunning."

Bryce refocused her eyes and had to admire the shape the dress seemed to bring out. It cinched at the waist, hugging her sides, and sweeping folds of fabric came across her chest, gathering on one shoulder. Gabby always seemed to know what would look good on Bryce.

"You really are."

She looked at Gabby. At the sight of her face filling with a trembling smile, Bryce had to smile back.

Gabby gave a quiet laugh. "You're going to steal him back from me in that."

Bryce's stomach balled up at the joke. Gabby drew in a breath but said nothing more, looking at Bryce, searching for her reaction.

Bryce remembered waiting her turn at the bottom of the ladder at practice as Gabby climbed ahead, wishing with every ounce that she would nail the dive every time. And Gabby always went first in the diving order because she could tell Bryce was nervous, though Bryce never said so. Gabby knew Bryce better than anybody. Some things mattered over time, but maybe this didn't. Maybe it shouldn't.

"Never," Bryce responded, shaking her head. "Never."

CHAPTER TEN

That night, Bryce got out of Gabby's car, and a deep, melodic buzzing filled her ears. The air belonged to the cicadas now, there was no doubt about that. They were creatures of the summer, sometimes called July flies. Bryce had always liked that name.

Inside, she found her father snoring on a reclining chair in front of the last inning of a Texas Rangers game. Next to him, on the floor, her mother breathed heavily, doing bicycle sit-ups, an old portable CD player blaring Electric Light Orchestra in her headphoned ears. At least they were in the same room. Her father barely left the den these days, and her mother was always in her office. Sydney was upstairs, music blaring from underneath her closed door.

Bryce made her way to the basement and tossed her shopping bags onto her bed. Aside from a few dressier diversions Gabby had convinced her to pursue, Bryce had stocked up on her usual V-necks, tank tops, and shorts with pockets.

She opened a drawer of the oval-shaped dresser, only to see it was full: her diving trophies. She felt a pang in her chest. One by one, she lined them up in height order, hanging medals around the gold cups and cylinders that topped each one.

When she leaned to shut the drawer, the edge of something silvery caught her eye. As she opened the drawer farther, she gasped. *The tiara.* Bryce brought out the worn silver crown, delicately woven with light-pink crystals, and let out a laugh of surprise.

When they were in first grade, the year after Gabby's father died, Gabby's mom, Elena, had taken them to a flea market. In one of the bargain bins, Gabby found a tiara. Not just a plastic, painted tiara like you would find in a toy store. A *real* tiara. The flea market clerk noticed its worth, too, and priced it high. Gabby's mother refused; money was tight, and Gabby's birthday had already passed. But Bryce's *own* birthday was coming up, and Elena had told Bryce she could pick something out for her present. When she encountered the small, circular package in the brightly wrapped pile of gifts, Bryce didn't even unwrap it. She immediately handed it to her friend. They spent most of that year playing Princess and Prince, Gabby wearing the crown and Bryce fighting imaginary dragons.

Bryce hung it on one of the tallest trophies, happiness swelling inside her. She'd invite Gabby over one of these days and casually motion to the dresser. She couldn't wait to see the look of surprise on her friend's face.

There. She stood back. The monochrome room felt more like hers again, the sparkling tiara and gilded plastic of each prize adding a gold glow to the gray corner.

Just little things, Bryce thought. She could move things little by little to get them back where they were supposed to be. Right? The coma was big. Not diving was big. The wedding would be big. But she could inch back in small ways, running errands with Gabby, talking to Sydney, taking back her room.

Like that window. Her mother must have cracked it to air the room out, and the cicadas' sounds floated in, their buzzing now hard and wild as the night grew darker. Bryce walked over to it and pressed on the frame, bringing the glass pane down.

And there it was. Her face reflected against the darkness, surprisingly clear. It had changed along with her body, in many of the same ways Gabby's face had changed. More defined features, vague lines that appeared when she moved her formerly round cheeks.

As she was about to turn away, Bryce noticed a light come on at the back of the property. Someone was in the barn.

She made her way outside. The night dripped with insect noise, and she could feel the tall grasses break beneath her boots. The buzzing was so loud now—she couldn't remember a time when the cicadas made so much noise. When she approached the barn, she saw a bike leaned against the red-painted doors. A familiar-looking bike. Bryce went inside.

He sat facing away from her on a wooden sawhorse, a camping lantern sitting on the floor beside him.

"Greg," she said.

He turned, his mouth opening in surprise, as if he hadn't expected to see her there.

"What are you doing here?" Bryce found her fists tightening, but not in anger. It was to get a grasp on what was happening. Her head began to spin.

Greg turned all the way around. His eyes bored deeply into hers. "Same thing I've been doing here forever."

The memories flooded her at the sight of him, biting his nails, his long legs on either side of the sawhorse.

They crashed into her like rapid-fire waves: he and Bryce,

on the same seat, legs intertwining. Bryce sneaking up on him as he faced away from her, kissing where his shoulder met his neck. The taste of his mouthwash. Climbing aboard her dad's propjet, seated beside one another, pretending to fly. Planning where they would go. Curling up in sleeping bags and falling asleep together, waking up just in time to sneak back into the house, the sky turning pink.

But now the wooden beams had a layer of dust an inch thick. The plane her father had been building was covered with an old blue tarp, his tools all put away. He used to work on it every day during his lunch hour. He was going to finish before Bryce went off to college. He had promised. It stood hulking, unfinished, beside Greg like the skeleton of some big animal. It was déjà vu, but all wrong.

"I came here when I was missing you," Greg explained quietly.

"Oh," Bryce muttered, imagining him wandering around the dark barn by himself. Her head sparked in pain. She had seen that in her vision, hadn't she?

Greg stood up. "I missed you every goddamn day. I felt like . . ." He swallowed. "I didn't really get the chance to tell you at the restaurant."

Bryce breathed through her nose, thinly and calmly, as her eyes darted from his thick-lashed eyes to his broad chest to his veined forearms, twitching as he settled against a beam.

She tried to keep her voice steady. "Then why did you . . . give up on me?"

Greg stopped. His eyes turned to the ceiling for the answer, but when they returned to meet hers, they had the same pain she had seen when he was here alone. "If I had known for a second that there was a chance you were going to wake up, I would have waited. You know I would have."

"They said I wasn't going to," she filled in quietly.

"They said you would never wake up," Greg echoed. "So I just sort of clung to the memories."

Bryce nodded, thinking of one unseasonably warm Saturday night when she and Greg had lain next to one another with their hands behind their heads, Bryce in a sports bra and basketball shorts, Greg in his usual Carhartts cut off at the knee. "How do blind people dream?" he had asked her.

"I don't know," Bryce said slowly, pondering. She was staring at the slant of the barn ceiling, fading into darkness at the top. Occasionally the dark would rustle with the flight of bats or barn swallows. The light of their lantern only reached so far.

"Do they have dreams in sound?" Greg asked, his voice getting sleepy.

That night Bryce had dreamed of a world upside down, dripping in surreal colors. Greg was leading her through it with her hand in his. They had floated through the air like it was made of water. Bryce felt right at home.

Now she felt tears burn in the corner of her eyes. "Memories weren't good enough, though." It was both a question and an answer.

"No," he said hollowly. "I moved on to these little dream scenarios. I wanted them to be real. I wanted it so bad. . . ." His voice choked. He looked away, shaking his head. "I thought about you opening your eyes. I stared at your face, *willing* you to open your eyes. Then you'd get up and we would leave the hospital together, we would go back to school, we'd graduate. Go to Vandy. And after that . . ." His voice trailed off, but his eyes said the rest. They contained an eternity. Where they would go, who they could be.

He was close enough that she could smell the wet wood scent that lingered on his clothes. He was inches away, and yet she couldn't touch him. She couldn't even hold his hand.

"Well, that's not how it is," Bryce said, ripping the words from her chest. She saw hurt flicker in Greg's eyes. "It doesn't matter how it could have been. You're with Gabby now. You're getting married."

Bryce felt something crack inside of her. The last time

she had said that word, *married*, had been in this barn. Their cheeks were red. Their hair was messed. The cicadas buzzed as they were buzzing now, and they had said silly, stupid things to each other. Love was being able to say anything you wanted, to say all the stupid things you couldn't tell anyone else. But she had meant that one.

"I know," Greg said sadly. Angrily, almost.

"I'm going to bed," she said.

"Don't," he said. "Stay."

But he didn't protest when Bryce walked back into the summer night, trying to catch her breath. When she turned back, the light still shone from the barn's old diamond-shaped windows. But she only looked ahead as she stepped through the wet grass, looking forward, for the first time since she awoke, to the soft darkness of a dreamless sleep.

CHAPTER ELEVEN

Bryce hung half out of the passenger-side window of the speeding white Honda. The rush of wind bit at her, flicking hair across her face, her mouth. This was a new kind of wind. It had a presence, a weight; it seemed to move like the bleeding colors only Bryce could see. She could feel it slip through her fingers and hair like liquid.

"Okay, here comes a big hill!" Bryce called to Carter, her knee braced on the busted leather seat.

He rolled his eyes, but a smile played on his lips.

"Go fast! It's like a roller coaster!"

"You look like my dog," he answered, but as soon as the

words were out, the engine gunned and Bryce let out a whoop as they broke the crest of the hill, the skin of her cheeks pulled back by the air whipping across the empty country road.

The pavement flattened out, and Bryce flopped back onto her seat. "I can't believe you let me do that."

Carter scoffed. "Me neither. We're lucky another car didn't come by."

"No cars ever do." Bryce pulled her wild locks back into a ponytail and hung her hand out the window, catching the warm wind with her palm.

Carter shook his head, looking forward, but unable to hide his smile. "You're crazy," he muttered.

"Sorry," Bryce said, but she wasn't.

"You know where we're going, right?" He readjusted the mirror.

"I couldn't get lost if I wanted to."

It had been a week since the night in the barn with Greg. He'd been calling, but she never picked up. It would be better to forget the past, she'd decided. It was better for both of them.

Carter had been coming around more often, and that was nice. But she found herself bringing him to all the places she used to go with Greg and Gabby, staring at the seats of the diner where they used to eat before practice, or searching for their faces at the mall, longing for them. Longing for a life that didn't exist anymore.

The asphalt gave way to the crackle of unpaved road. "Pull up under this tree," she said. It'd be strange to be at the lake without Greg and Gabby, but she had put off going for too long. Never had this much time passed in the summer before Bryce took a trip out to Percy. She couldn't wait to see it, to feel the smooth, warm water. It was more pure than chlorine water. The lake's algae was dark and slimy, but to Bryce it felt right. The lake was *alive*.

A single path led to a small, dirty beach scattered with a couple coal-streaked grills and empty beer cans. Bryce hadn't been to that beach since she was a kid. She grabbed Carter's hand and pulled him off the beaten path, through the grass and ferns and tiny saplings, to a hedge of bushes and trees that hid the rest of the lake from view.

"Wow," Carter said, making his fingers into a picture frame. "What a view."

"Shut up," she said, but they were both smiling. "I have a spot. It's the perfect spot."

She crept along the thick row of trees, peeking between them only to see more trees, more leaves. Over the past week, her legs had gotten stronger and stronger. She could almost walk normally now. Every step burned, but she relished the sore-muscle feeling. "Now I just have to remember where the opening is."

Every so often she would stop, staring into the bushes, but she could tell that wasn't the right way. She didn't know how, because everything looked the same, but she could tell.

"It's okay if you can't remember, you know," Carter called up at one point. "It *has* been five years of brain inactivity."

"Doesn't feel that way," Bryce breathed to herself. Sweat began to drip from her forehead as they rustled along. She didn't mind; it was good to be moving.

Suddenly, as if the trees were breathing a sigh of relief, they broke into a clearing. Bushes still dotted the grass, but beyond them lay nothing but a single, mangled crabapple tree, and the lake and sky in two shades of endless blue.

"Look." Bryce rushed to the edge of the clearing and motioned for Carter. "The bank juts straight down so it's really deep. With a cliff to dive off and everything."

Bryce watched Carter take it all in. Even in his white Oxford and khaki pants, he seemed to belong here more than anyone she had seen. Gabby usually took this opportunity to apply suntan lotion, and Greg always scrambled down the bluff to jump in without a second look. But Carter was completely still, his blue-gray eyes drinking in the view without a word.

After a while he looked at Bryce, his eyes moving up and

down her face. She felt herself blushing. "I didn't bring a swimsuit," he said absently.

"Oh." Bryce cleared her throat. "Me neither." A pang of loss hit her. "I don't even know if I can swim anymore."

They collapsed under the crab apple tree, Bryce letting out a grateful moan to get out of the beating sun. She stared through the maze of branches to the blue sky above.

"You ever seen one of these trees in the spring?" she asked, gesturing up to the berrylike crab apples.

"Yeah," he said, grinning. "They blossom in these really pretty pink flowers."

Bryce laughed at his enthusiasm.

Carter cleared his throat. "I mean, right? That's what they do?" But then he let out a small laugh with her. "No, I know them well. My little brother used to climb up the ones on our street when the apples came in, throw 'em down, try to peg me." He threw the grass he had pulled up in his hand, scattering the blades in the breeze.

"I used to do the same thing to my little sister," Bryce remembered.

"Chucking apples at someone younger than you? That's hardly fair." Carter took this opportunity to grab a handful of crab apples and toss them at Bryce, one by one.

Bryce retaliated with a few apples of her own, trying to

land them in the collar of his shirt. "I wish I could throw something at her now. She could use some sense knocked into her."

Carter surrendered, blocking her aim with his shoulder. "Why? What's she doing?"

"You've seen her." Bryce chucked a crab apple toward the bluff.

Carter contemplated. "She's probably just going through a stage."

"Whatever," Bryce grunted, launching apples further with each throw. "That's not the point."

"What is—" Carter started to ask.

Bryce stopped throwing. "The point is my parents totally dropped the ball." She was getting frustrated now. Carter had seen her family plenty. He had to know what she was talking about. "She goes out every night looking like a baby prostitute. She comes home at three in the morning."

"But she does come home."

"So? She doesn't get good grades. She doesn't play any sports or do any activities. And my parents just sit around, moping about it, not doing anything."

Carter shrugged. "Maybe it's beyond their control."

"You think?" Bryce asked sarcastically.

She stood up, wiping dirt and grass off of her butt. Carter looked up at her thoughtfully.

"You know, just because she's not a star . . ." He trailed off, gesturing to her. "It doesn't mean she's a failure."

Bryce smirked, kicking at the dirt. "Oh, sure, she's a real winner."

The sun was officially fading now, setting the few long, streaky clouds on fire.

"I want to go home," Bryce muttered.

"If you say so. I say we're missing the best part." He nodded toward the sunset. Bryce wandered to the edge of the bluff, away from him, arms folded. What did he know about the best part? This was her lake.

They watched the deep blue of evening take over the sky. Then, without waiting, she took the lead, and soon they were back on the empty country road, gliding home through the cool air.

She could tell Carter was sneaking glances at her, still silent. When she happened to glance at him, his gaze was steeled ahead, one arm on the wheel. Thirty minutes later, they pulled up to Bryce's house.

"Bye," Bryce said, unbuckling her seat belt. "Thanks for the field trip."

"Yeah. See you soon." His eyebrows knit together as he clutched the steering wheel. "Hey, Bryce?"

"What?" She ducked back inside the car.

"Go easy on them, okay?" He nodded toward her house. Bryce felt herself tense. "You don't know what it's like to lose someone you love that way."

"And *you* don't know what it's like to lose five years of your life." She closed the door and he drove off.

As she made her way up the lawn, fuming, the automatic light from the driveway illuminated to reveal the open garage door and Sydney with a can of gold spray paint in her hand.

"Moved on to vandalism now?" Bryce called. Sydney looked up.

A pair of vintage high tops sat on a paint-splattered sheet on the cement. Bryce couldn't tell what their original color was, but now they were a deep, shiny gold.

"Don't touch those," Sydney said in greeting, taking off one of their dad's oversized Vanderbilt T-shirts and tossing it onto the cement floor.

"Why were you messing up Dad's shirt?" Bryce asked, grabbing it from the ground.

"Chill, Bryce. I was using it to protect my clothes."

Sydney wore a completely sheer lace dress, her black bra and spandex boy shorts visible underneath. Her feet were tucked into impossibly high chunky heels, and she had put a thick black ring through her lip piercing. Bryce snorted. "Ha. Clothes. Good one."

A rusty blue car without a muffler pulled up in front of the Graham residence. The side was emblazoned with the graphic B60 and it was being driven by an emaciated-looking guy with bleached hair and a tattoo sleeve. He revved his engine, echoing off the soft-lit houses, and shouted at Sydney to hurry her ass up.

Sydney grabbed her purse from the ground.

"Who is that guy?" Bryce squinted to get a closer look.

Sydney adjusted her painted face briefly in a compact mirror and said casually, "Like you care?" She snapped the compact shut.

Bryce's fists clenched. As Sydney made her way down the driveway, Bryce had the urge to topple her tall, skinny form over like a mannequin. The B60 zoomed off, engine roaring. After a minute, the street was quiet again.

In a fury, Bryce picked up one of Sydney's spray-painted shoes and hurled it as hard as she could toward the grass.

"I do care," she said aloud. But there was no one there to hear her.

CHAPTER TWELVE

Y ou know I hate surprises, Dad." Bryce followed her father from her bedroom to the basement storage room the next evening.

"Just wait, you're gonna love it." It took her dad several kicks to get the storage door open, but when he did, Bryce gasped.

All the boxes were gone. Rubber mats covered the unfinished floor, and on top of the mats stood a full rack of free weights, medicine balls, and a large piece of equipment that could transition from an elliptical to a rowing machine. The sole piece of decoration hung under one of the high, small windows: a *Rocky* poster. Sylvester Stallone's gray sweat-suited form seemed to nod back at her in appreciation.

Her father put his hands on his hips proudly. His gold shirt with the Vanderbilt logo was tucked neatly into his pants, and a speck of shaving cream still hung near where his close-cropped hair met his neck. "Started installing it when you came home."

"Wow." Bryce stepped up to wrap her hand around a free weight. She picked it up. The metal was cool to the touch, and the weight of it jerked her weak arm down. She set it back on the rack and closed her eyes, letting memories overtake her.

She remembered putting one foot in front of the other on the rough, bright turquoise board. Pushing off her left, her head leading her body, limbs tight but relaxed. The world seemed to rotate around her as she stayed still in the air. For a millisecond that contained an eternity, she was weightless. Flying. Then she snapped, tight, and straightened, ready to break the surface. When she hit the water, her sight was a dark kaleidoscope. Her body hung in suspense in the water, then flew upward.

She broke for air on the sunny day, hitting the water with her fist, her dad shouting in celebration.

"Perfect!" He shouted. "REVERSE! Two and a half!" he yelled, pausing between each word, like a football announcer calling a touchdown. "SOMERSAULT! TUCK!"

She swam over and gave him a high five.

At the snap of the two hands, Bryce opened her eyes to the workout room, her father beside her. It was the dive she'd done when she hit her head. The dive she was *supposed* to do.

"Things didn't work out the way we planned, did they?"

Her father gave her a long look. "No, they didn't." He took a breath, but then didn't say anything else.

Bryce shivered. "It must have been hard."

"Yeah." He nodded. "Your old man wasn't really sure what to do with himself when he wasn't yelling at you all the time." He chuckled, but the sound caught in his throat.

Bryce pretended to be occupied by picking up a medicine ball. She pressed it from her chest. "I know," she said. "I saw the plane." She thought of its still, silent form sitting in the unused barn. *You stopped doing everything. Working. Coaching. Living.* "Still not done."

He nodded wordlessly and looked away, blinking. He was blinking back tears, she realized.

He dabbed at his eyes with his wrist, gesturing around the room. "I thought about making it more like your physical therapy room at the hospital, but then I remembered those mornings at the Y. . . ."

When Bryce made the Tennessee AAU team in eighth

grade, her father had driven her to the Nashville Y to lift weights most mornings before school. Bryce had hated it at first, groaning and snapping at her dad as he pulled her out of bed, even crying some days from the fatigue, but then he would say, "Okay. Go back to sleep. If you want to skip today, that's fine." She would stay silent, then, pulling on her sweatshirt, and walk ahead of him out to the car.

He turned her to face him now, both hands on her shoulders. "It's not going to be easy."

Bryce just nodded. She still resented her dad for not telling her that he'd stopped coaching. For spending every night holed up in the den. But then she looked around the room. It said everything that he couldn't. That he was sorry for what happened. That he never meant to push her so hard. That he needed to get back to normal just as badly as she did.

Finally, she smiled, putting her hands on his. "You know me too well."

Five minutes later, Bryce was in a Hilwood High T-shirt and shiny blue athletic shorts. She sat at the rowing machine, trying to keep her knobby knees from pressing together, gripping and regripping the handles to find the perfect fit.

She pushed her body backward off the metal plate by straightening her legs, yanking the bands with her. Her thigh muscles were already trembling. Her shoulders cried out with the effort. She clenched her jaw against the pain and smiled up at her dad.

"Thatta girl," he said. "We'll make the first goal five."

Warmth ran through Bryce's veins. Maybe it was the endorphins, maybe it was just muscle strain, but Bryce got a special pleasure from working out. It was her drug, and her dad had just provided her with unlimited doses.

"Unh!" she grunted, shooting her body backward, again yanking the rowing bands. She held the tension for a millisecond, then let go as she poised for another rep.

"Can we do this every day?" she asked her dad breathlessly.

"That's the idea," he answered.

She used to train *twice* a day. Mornings in the weight room, afternoons in the pool. Bryce shot back for another rep, watching her puny quads ball up under her shorts and release, feeling now like they were going to detach from the bone.

"Maybe we could make long-term goals, too," Bryce panted. "Try to get my PRs back to what they were."

"Bryce? Are you down here?" Bryce's mother's voice came down the stairs. A moment later she entered, holding a mug of steaming tea. She took in the miniature workout center with her eyebrows raised. "What is this?" she asked slowly.

"*This* . . ." Bryce's father said, "is a gift for my daughter."

Bryce's mother's knuckles whitened around her mug. Her

darting eyes rested on the *Rocky* poster. "You did all this without talking to me first?"

"It's just some basic stuff."

"You really think she's in a condition to use all this?" her mother said tersely. "She has a CAT scan tomorrow, by the way."

Her mother turned to Bryce. "Bryce, your laundry is *still* on the dryer."

Bryce nodded, taking the hint. With her head down, she made her way out the door, grabbing the clean clothes on her way to her room. But her mother's voice didn't leave her.

"You can't help yourself, can you?" she hissed.

Bryce's head shot up. There were now two walls and a large room between her and her parents, but she could hear them as if they were right next to her. She wanted to cover her ears, or to move further away, but she knew somehow that it would make no difference.

"Do you *want* her to have a relapse? You heard what the doctor said. I'm not going to let you push her like you did before."

Alone in her room, Bryce cringed. She could feel the words echo in her skull.

"Goddamnit, Beth." Her father spoke in hardly more than a whisper. She always knew he was angry when his voice got that quiet. "I get it. I almost killed our daughter. You haven't let me forget that in five years. But for god's sake, let me help her get better."

"I'm just trying to—"

"Would you just have her stay inside all day, never try and get back to normal?"

"No, but . . ." Her mother's voice choked. "We're supposed to be a team."

Bryce sat on her bed, feeling sick. They weren't a team anymore. Her accident had split them in two. And her recovery was pushing them further apart.

She heard her father scoff. "Wow, Beth, you were really thinking of the *team* when you took on a thousand clients and turned our house into your office."

Bryce broke away to the small bathroom next to her room and turned on the faucet, letting the roar of the water drown her parents out, dabbing at the tears that were beginning to form in the corners of her eyes. When she came back into her room, she saw her phone was lit up with missed calls and text messages. They were all from Greg.

pls pick up bry. we need to talk.

Another missed call after that. And then:

meet me tonite? arboretum @ midnight. i'll be waiting.

Bryce kept scrolling. There was one final message:

for as long as it takes.

Bryce nodded to the empty room, letting a single tear slide down her cheek.

✳

Her heart was pounding as she slid open the basement doors that night, tiptoeing around the pool, ducking through the tall grass. The route to the arboretum came to her as smoothly as a pike. That's what this was. Nothing but muscle memory.

All the houses on River Drive shared a "backyard" with a half acre of land set aside by the state of Tennessee to house rare species of trees. About a mile beyond Bryce's barn, off of County Road B, where dust broke through the pavement in cracks, the leaves of threatened trees shivered behind a wrought-iron fence. Plaques were driven in the dirt in front of each type—AFRICAN TEAK, RED SANDALWOOD, WEST INDIAN CEDAR. When she was five, the arboretum had just been sanctioned, and the trees were only inches taller than she was. Now people got married in the dappled light, kids played hide and seek behind the trunks, and older couples rested in the shade.

Tonight it was empty. Bryce had to suck in sideways to squeeze between the iron bars. She wandered between the rows, listening for Greg. It was ten past midnight. Maybe he had decided not to come. Bryce's thoughts swam in the warm hush.

Here, midnight, five years ago, Bryce had watched Greg smoke a cigarette he took from his dad's glove compartment. The ice packs strapped to their shoulders after practice had long ago melted. Greg had taken the cigarette out of his pocket on the walk from the barn, saying he had been saving it to celebrate the shittiest practice he had all year. He wanted to punish his body, he said. Bryce refused to get within ten feet of him.

That night, they walked parallel with two rows of trees between them, Bryce kicking dead dandelions, trying not to look at Greg surrounded by smoke.

"Admit it," he called to her through the dark. "I look sexy. I look like the Marlboro Man."

Bryce answered by grabbing her throat and gagging.

"It's really not bad," he said, and a fiery dot appeared briefly in the air. He exhaled and said, "Better than the stupid clove cigarettes Tommy Orr made me try that time."

Bryce stopped, squinting at the cloudy figure she could barely make out between the skinny lines of young trees. "Better than fresh air? I doubt it."

"Oh, Bryce," he said, stamping out the cigarette on the sole of his Nikes. "You're so pure."

Then he had zigzagged his way through the trunks and

kissed her gently on the mouth. It was true, what they said; he tasted like an ashtray. But surprisingly, Bryce didn't mind it. Greg never smoked again.

"Sorry I'm late."

Bryce glanced up. Her eyes found his form in the dark. Greg's chiseled torso was visible under his polo shirt. He sidestepped to lean back on a tree, his hands in his pockets.

"That's okay," Bryce said. She lifted her chin. "So what are we doing here?"

"We need to talk."

Bryce stepped closer to him. *We did talk,* she wanted to say. But she stopped herself. "Okay," she said. "So . . ."

"Well," he started, rubbing his chin. "There's a problem when you're supposed to get married and an ex-girlfriend is—"

"Ex-girlfriend?" The term was like a lemon in her mouth. But that's what she was, wasn't she?

"Not like that," he started again slowly. "It's just hard to explain to a girl who is looking at me like she was in my arms yesterday."

"Oh, really? *I'm* the one stuck in the past? How about you just showing up in my barn?"

Greg stepped away from the tree, toward Bryce. "I'm not saying I don't do the same thing. I look at you the same way, I know that."

"Yeah." Bryce nodded. "You do."

He sighed. "How could I not? You're even more beautiful to me now, if that's possible."

Bryce's hands shot up to her face. She pressed on her cheeks, as if to push the emotions away. "What would Gabby think if she heard you say that?"

"Gabby," he said. He looked at the ground. "It's complicated, Bry."

He looked up slowly, putting his hands in his pockets. He always seemed so relaxed as he stepped on the diving platform. He stepped toward her the same way now.

"It wasn't that Gabby and I weren't thinking of you when . . ." He paused, looking for words. "When we started to be together."

Bryce couldn't help but say tensely, "I doubt that." If they had thought of her, she wouldn't be standing across from Greg tonight, the distance separating them. He would have been right there with her when she woke up, holding her hand.

"Bryce, you—your accident is *why* we're together."

"Oh, great," Bryce said, her voice shaking.

"I don't mean it like that. I mean, it brought us together. We were the only two people who knew what it was like to really miss you." He sighed loudly. "If you hadn't gone out of my life, there's no way I would be with Gabby."

Bryce stayed silent. The trees were dark silhouettes against the moonglow of an overcast night. Crickets sang. Cicadas sang louder.

Greg took a breath. "Five years were stolen from you, Bryce. And in a way, it was stolen from me, too." Then he finished, sounding strained for the first time. "From us."

He took her hand. She started to shake, thinking of something to say.

But by the time the words came to her, he had pressed his lips to hers. She felt a tingling down her back and the warmth of his arms. Just this once, she told herself, but with her mouth on his, her hands on his neck, moving down to his shoulders, tasting him taste her, her mind became as blank and flat as the sky.

She stopped shaking.

When the caress of Greg's lips became soft enough for air, Bryce stepped back. His breath was hot on her cheek. Should she kiss him again? She stood on the brink of the next move, like a platform. Feet on stone, skin feeling the endless potential for contact, complete submersion one step away . . .

Bryce dove back in.

CHAPTER THIRTEEN

Walking was walking. Bryce didn't even have to think about it anymore. She moved across the rubber floor of the Vanderbilt physical therapy room with all eyes on her.

"Bravo, Bryce!" Jane was loudest of all of them. She stood with a few other nurses Bryce recognized, Dr. Warren, and her parents.

Bryce had walked a straight line back and forth from one end of the room to the other, and then she had walked another line, faster, and another one, faster than that.

"This is truly remarkable, Bryce," Dr. Warren said kindly.

Jane stepped over to give Bryce an enthusiastic rub on the shoulder. "Do you know how lucky you are, missy?"

"She's not lucky, she's a Graham," her father called from behind the group, and Bryce couldn't help but roll her eyes.

Dr. Warren smiled politely. "Very impressive."

"Yeah, so . . . are all these scans and tests really necessary?" Bryce was pushing now, she knew that.

"I'm afraid so."

Dr. Warren ushered Bryce to the waiting room. It had one window and smelled like medicine and cleaner, and here she was supposed to wait for a doctor to tell her that she was physically incapable of living a normal life.

She curled up in the chair.

"I heard it was a good show in there." Carter sat next to her, smelling like clean clothes, holding two smoothies. They hadn't talked since their trip to Percy Lake, and she felt guilty for ignoring him. "I accidentally bought an extra smoothie, so you can have this one if you want."

Bryce's mother looked up from a crossword and smiled at Carter.

Bryce buried herself deeper into the rough fabric of the chairs. "Nobody *accidentally* buys an extra smoothie."

"Okay." Carter looked exasperated. "I bought a smoothie just for you. Do you want it or not?"

Bryce's dad snorted from behind his *ESPN* magazine.

"Yes," Bryce said begrudgingly, and sat up.

But before she could get her lips around the straw, Jane appeared in the waiting room in her Garfield scrubs, her glasses on a chain around her neck. She summoned the Grahams.

"Wipe that look off your face, hon," she said to Bryce cheerily. "It's time to get your brain looked at."

Inside the machine, Bryce could barely hear Dr. Warren's directions to stay as still as possible. It was like Bryce was underwater and Dr. Warren was calling from above the surface. The problem was that Bryce wasn't used to keeping still in the water; she was used to moving through it.

The mechanical bed came to a stop in the middle of a wide plastic tube. She was encased. She could barely breathe.

Bryce panicked, her eyes darting around the gray plastic walls surrounding her, inches from her face. There was a stinging heat behind her neck. They said it wouldn't hurt. Why did it hurt? The pain spread to the familiar spot in her forehead, wrapping around her skull. *Oh no.*

It hurt worse than before. Her hands went numb. Her feet, too. She should stop the procedure. She tried to lift her head. Hopefully Dr. Warren would notice the movement. But then suddenly she wasn't in the machine anymore.

A car with no muffler, speeding down the street.

Music with heavy bass was blaring, and a person next to her was laughing, her hair falling around her face. The car was full of people laughing. Something about it was not right. The music was too loud, or the people were too happy, something was off. Everything was sharper than it should be.

They stopped at a light, and Bryce had a terrible sinking feeling.

She tried to get the attention of the dark-haired person next to her, who was whipping her head to the beat, leaning and rocking to the bass. "Something's wrong—" Bryce shouted, but her voice didn't exist. She didn't exist. It was as if she was pressed against glass, a one-way mirror where nobody could see her.

The scene froze, and Bryce watched the laughing faces as lightning seared across her skull again.

She saw red, red, and nothing but red.

When the lightning stopped, Bryce opened her eyes. She was awake on the vinyl bed, the scanner pushed back, and her mother, father, and Dr. Warren surrounded her, making sounds she couldn't make out.

"I'm okay," she said immediately, making sure to keep her eyes ahead. The pain was leaving, the heat was leaving, and in its place was the same strange clarity that filtered her vision when she first woke up.

"Sorry, I fell asleep. I think I had a nightmare." She waited for the numbness to fade.

Her parents nodded with knit brows as Bryce slowly sat up, but Dr. Warren tried to ease her gently down.

She looked more flustered than Bryce had ever seen her. "Just, just one second, here, Bryce. Let me see if we can get any results, and we'll go back to my office."

Bryce let herself breathe shallow, openmouthed breaths, ignoring the image still painted on the back of her eyelids, the bright car full of laughter.

*

Dr. Warren's office looked exactly the same, not a pen or paper out of place. She loomed behind her desk, gesturing to the Graham family to pull up chairs. Bryce preferred to stand.

The doctor ran her hands through her gray strands, then set them flat on the desk. Bryce heard them hit the wood with a dull slap. She shook the sound away.

"This is a difficult situation. The scan results are unclear. We're going to try to see what we can salvage from them, but they're . . . they're confusing. I'm afraid we're going to need to keep you here for observation, Bryce."

"No!" Bryce cried. "No," she said again. Her eyes darted toward the door. Something strange had happened to her, she knew that. It would keep happening. And she couldn't let them find out. They would never let her leave.

Carter knocked, entering the office. "Still no clear results," he said. He looked at Bryce, sensing tension in the room.

"See? This is pointless." She threw up her hands.

But Dr. Warren wouldn't give up. "I just wonder how much toll returning to the real world has had on your stress reflexes. I couldn't get results, but I could tell you were in pain, Bryce. Perhaps your recovery time could be spent in a less stimulating environment. Maybe not here, but a retreat of some sort . . ."

The doctor looked at Bryce's parents for approval.

Bryce stepped in between them. "I won't. I'll take more meds if you want."

"That's not exactly what I meant," Dr. Warren said.

"I've had enough of this. I'm sorry. I've just—I've just had enough." Bryce walked out of the office, bracing herself to push past anyone who would stop her. No one did.

On instinct, Bryce grabbed her phone from her pocket, her finger poised over Greg's name. She couldn't call him, could she? What had happened at the arboretum was a one-time thing. Just once, and it wasn't going to happen again. She couldn't let it happen again.

But then she pictured driving and driving until everything receded in the distance. Until her problems were far enough away to feel small and insignificant.

Can you come get me? she typed. *Back entrance of hospital ASAP.*

Immediately after she closed it, her phone vibrated.

c ya in 10.

She weaved through the halls, trying to lose herself in the hospital's winding corridors. She walked and walked, but everything about the hallways was familiar—the fluorescent lights, the incessant beeping of machines, the cacophony of TVs mixing from different rooms, and then the sight of Carter standing beside a bed, silhouetted by the light.

Past him, a little boy with dark hair lay motionless. He looked peaceful, like he was taking a nap.

Carter looked up, meeting her gaze. "What are you doing here? No one knew where you went."

Bryce gestured to the boy in the bed. "How long has he been here?"

"Too long," he replied shortly.

"How?" Bryce asked. There was nothing else to say.

"Car accident," he said flatly. "Head trauma." His whole face twitched, as if the words hurt him physically.

Bryce looked closer at the boy. That dark hair. The high forehead. "Is that your brother?"

Carter nodded. "Sam," he said. Their eyes met. There was a deep sadness in his voice. It all hit Bryce in a rush. Why Carter spent so much time in the neurology wing. Why he was so adamant she go easy on her family. *You don't know what it's like to lose someone you love that way.* It was true; she didn't know. But he did.

Bryce felt ready to collapse. She was spent. "I'm so sorry," she said. "I have to go."

She found the back entrance, near the Dumpsters where the nurses went on cigarette breaks, and folded up against the smoke-stained wall. She counted in her head to avoid thinking about what happened in the CAT scan machine, to avoid wondering what would happen now. *1, 2, 3, 4 . . .* At *14*, Carter reappeared.

"Don't worry." He sat next to her. "I won't tell anyone you're here."

She didn't respond. *15, 16, 17.*

"You really should go back to your parents, though. They're still in the office, waiting for you." He turned to her. "You know, Dr. Warren can't force you to do anything. I don't know why you go so crazy."

The counting stopped. She couldn't tell him about the

visions, about the strange and beautiful way the world looked now. She couldn't even tell herself about the visions. What they were. Why they came. Bryce sighed. "I don't want to talk about it."

"Okay." It was easy as that. "Do you want a ride home? I can tell them you want time alone."

"Nah," Bryce said. "Just tell them I'll meet them back at the house later on."

Carter leaned closer to her, as if he were about to whisper something in her ear. Then he wrapped his arms around her. Being close to him, Bryce felt the urge to dissolve, to crumble into pieces and float away, little by little. It was nothingness, but also relief.

"Hey," called a voice. Greg. He'd pulled up across the street.

Carter let go, looking at her with his brow furrowed.

"He's taking me to see Gabby," Bryce said automatically. "I'll see you later."

"Yeah," Carter said as they helped each other up.

Bryce opened the car door, then turned back to him. "See you."

"Okay."

She got in and slammed the door, watching Carter's frame grow smaller in the rearview mirror as they drove away.

CHAPTER FOURTEEN

Where to?" Greg said, his eyes ahead.

Bryce peeled her eyes from the mirror, breathing in the smell of air freshener hanging near the air conditioner. She pushed the OFF button and rolled down the window, closing her eyes as the breeze played on her face.

"Anywhere," she said, leaning her head back on the brown leather headrest.

Over the rumble of his engine, Bryce heard him drawl, "If we could really go anywhere, I'd drive us down to Louisiana. Get one of those boats with fans on the back and float through the swamps. All the way down the gulf. Sleep in a hut hanging over the marshlands. Wake up and eat shrimp straight out of the water."

"Louisiana in the summer, Greg?" Bryce chuckled, her eyes still closed. "It'd be like walking through an armpit."

Still, she imagined it. Greg posed like a pirate at the front of the flat boat as it chugged through the moss and the reeds, his bare back golden brown, shining, his T-shirt tied around his head to soak up the sweat.

They drove for miles and miles, and Bryce let herself be lulled by the steady motion of the car. She was surprised when the truck slowed down outside of a long, manicured driveway, and they pulled into the parking lot of a golf course. A gilded metal sign read WHISPERING PINES.

Bryce got out of the truck, looking out over the hoods of expensive cars. "What, you want to hit a few balls?"

"Nah," Greg said, coming around the side of the truck to stand with her. He stripped off his pale blue polo and tossed it through the open window. He wore a gray Army T-shirt with the sleeves cut off, and Bryce felt her face grow hot. "Come on."

Bryce followed him along the fairway, ducking behind a long row of pines, hearing the golfers' shouts and laughter tinkling from the green. Finally they reached a slope covered in rocks.

Greg scaled down the slope with ease and waited for Bryce at the dusty bottom, sandstone surrounding them on both sides. "You're never gonna guess where this goes."

The deep V of rocks went on for some time. Bryce watched her footing as they went, the sandstone dust staining the red of her boots. Suddenly the sun's glare wasn't so strong.

She looked up. Thick metal slats crisscrossed above them, holding up a groaning metal bridge. Trees rose up where the rocks ended, close in color to the rust caked on the large circular bolts. She heard the sharp, sweet chirps of birds, with sparkling clarity. The shadows swirled around the lines of the bridge like ribbons.

"It's a riverbed," Greg said, his chest lifting and falling under the triangle of sweat at his collar. "Or at least, it was."

Bryce smiled, remembering all the places Greg had led her. She had grown to trust the peaceful expression on his face when he was looking for just the right place, like he was fixing something that was broken. She'd follow his figure even as he wriggled through holes in electric fences, so they could find what he deemed a perfect spot in some farmer's field. Once he found it, there was no fanfare; he would just sit down and pull grass out of the earth as he wondered aloud whether aliens existed, or if there was a spot on earth where no person had stood before. She always thought they were going to get caught trespassing, but they never did.

Bryce noticed tracks running across the bridge. "Do trains still run on this?"

"Never saw one before," Greg said, making his way toward Bryce. He stood with his shoulder almost touching hers, his arms crossed. "But it's been a long time since I've been out here."

"It's been a while since I've been anywhere," Bryce breathed, enjoying the dappled light on the sharp rocks, the way the bridge and the trees seemed to support each other. "Feels like I've spent my life in a hospital bed. I couldn't wait to get out of there."

"Funny," Greg said, chucking a rock down the empty riverbed as if skipping it. "You're always trying to get out of that hospital, while I always had trouble getting in."

Bryce raised her eyebrows in surprise as Greg told her how he almost got arrested trying to sneak into her hospital room after hours when they were seventeen.

"When you first got there your room was on the first floor, near the ICU. So when they tried to boot me one night when visiting hours were over, I climbed back in the window."

Bryce laughed. "Did it work?"

Greg grinned up at the bridge above them, remembering. "Yeah, no," he drawled. "It was the wrong window and the guy in there started screaming."

"I wish I could have seen that," Bryce laughed, her heart flooding. They climbed up to the edge of the riverbed, where the rocks met dry grass. They sat down beside each other, splaying out their feet.

Greg reached out to touch her cheek. "It was somethin'," he said.

"Greg." Bryce pulled away. "We can't."

He looked down. "I know, it's just . . ." Then he looked up, his eyes meeting hers. "What if we could?"

Bryce opened her mouth, then closed it, losing her words in his deep blue eyes and long lashes. *We should,* she thought. She felt whole here, with him. She wanted to be in his world of dry riverbeds and old bridges.

He turned toward Bryce, putting a hand on her shoulder. Her thoughts stopped. She didn't move a muscle. He was breathing through his nose, his lips turning up at the corners. His eyes found hers, then traveled down her face to her lips, then back up to her eyes.

"I missed you so much," he said, his voice almost a whisper, and his mouth connected with hers.

Bryce didn't pull away. Her blood coursed hotly through

her veins, matching the heat outside so that her skin blended into the wet air, the sun-soaked rocks.

Greg put his hands on her waist, tucking them under her shirt to find her bare skin. His lips made a path to her jaw, her ear, her neck. A sound rumbled at the edge of their hearing, growing in intensity as Bryce wrapped her arms around his back.

Suddenly it ripped past them, taking over all their senses, pulling them apart.

"A train!" Greg called over the roar and squeak of wheels over the track, and they lifted their eyes toward the metal blur.

When it had passed, Bryce and Greg looked at each other. In the sudden silence, she remembered herself.

"What's Gabby doing today?" she said, swallowing.

Greg scratched his head, looking uncomfortable. "She's with her grandparents out in Hendersonville."

Bryce nodded. Finally, she said quietly, "What do you really want, Greg?"

He dropped his eyes downward. "I don't know."

He leaned back on the dry grass and started talking up to the sky, almost as if Bryce wasn't there. "My parents—they're pretty excited I'm settling down. Moving to a big city with lots of jobs. They didn't even think I'd graduate. Hell, they didn't think I'd even make it to college."

Greg's family was originally from a tiny town a few hours from Nashville, out in the deep, deep country. He didn't have much money growing up. His parents didn't even have a TV. He and his brother spent most of their time on their bikes, finding little ponds to go for swims, or climbing trees. He took to diving as he took to every other sport, like he'd done it all his life. When his parents saw how crowds would gather to watch him do flips off the high dive at the community pool, they scraped their money together to move him to Nashville so he could practice with a real diving team.

"It's good that your mom and dad don't have to worry about you," Bryce said with a sad smile.

Greg shook his head. "I'm not saying . . ." He sat up. "Bryce, that was never really my dream. It was theirs, and it was Gabby's. I've never really known what I wanted." He blinked. "Except for you."

Bryce didn't move from his grasp. She wanted to go back to five minutes ago, before the train had hurtled through, breaking them apart. But the heat of kissing him had faded, and Bryce had begun to put dusty space between them, inch by inch. Space enough for the thought of Gabby to breeze through.

Greg's face was hopeful as he asked, "Maybe we could get away from here, go somewhere else?"

"But where? How would we live?" With all the rigidity of their training, performing flawless dive after flawless dive in a square pool of pristine water, Bryce understood why Greg craved looseness the way he did. But they couldn't just drive to Louisiana and float down a river. Life didn't work like that.

She saw the uncertainty creep back into Greg's face.

"You made a decision." She breathed in deeply. "You asked Gabby to marry you. You made plans to move to D.C. You can't just . . . undo that."

Greg was looking at her, his eyebrows knit together. "I couldn't do anything if I thought I wasn't going to see you again. Gabby or no Gabby. I couldn't get out of bed in the morning."

His eyes had a fear to them, a fear and a longing. "I could never not talk to you," Bryce said. "You were my boyfriend, but you were also my friend." She sighed, giving what she hoped was a reassuring smile. "Maybe that's all we can be now."

Greg just shook his head, stood, and chucked another rock down the empty riverbed. It skittered over the dry rocks. But he didn't argue or try to change her mind.

The sky began to pinken above them as they made their way back to the car. By the time they pulled onto River Drive, it had turned a midnight blue. The truck rolling to a stop in front of her house was almost a shock to Bryce. This would have been the point where Greg kissed her and told her to sneak out to meet him later in the barn. She would say *maybe, I've got homework,* but what she really meant was *yes.* Yes, of course. She always meant yes.

But Gabby was probably home from Hendersonville by now. She was probably calling Greg, wondering where he was. Bryce pushed open the truck door and hopped out of the cab.

Greg leaned toward her, hair falling in his eyes. He reached out his hand.

Bryce took it, squeezed, and matched her voice to the cool quiet. "'Bye, friend," she said, and then she let go.

CHAPTER FIFTEEN

Bryce's palm filled with a creamy, fluffy pile of mousse. Her hands shook as she rubbed them together, feeling the airy liquid ooze between her fingers. Gently, she applied it to her hair, scrunching the ends up to touch her roots, letting the blond strands fall, curlier than before.

Looking nice was important today. Looking put-together, like a person who could do five reps on the rowing machine without having to sit down in the shower afterward. Like a person who would accept that the past was the past, and that her boyfriend was no longer her boyfriend.

A few days ago, Gabby had called. "The three of us

should go bowling," she had said. "I need a break from fussing about the wedding."

"Are you sure?" Bryce had gulped as she stood by the pool in her pajamas. She was always in her pajamas these days, it seemed.

"Of course! We should have done this as soon as you woke up. It'll be just like old times."

Now she thought about calling Gabby and telling her she wasn't feeling well. How could she stand watching Gabby and Greg together? How could she face her friend when she could still feel the touch of his lips on hers? She had told him they should just be friends. But he would never feel like just a friend to her.

Bryce sighed. She had avoided Gabby long enough. So she rubbed some concealer on the sleepless bags under her eyes. She almost dropped the bottle, bobbling it in her hands, when she heard a knock at the front door.

Bryce yanked her skirt down a few inches and emerged from the hall bathroom. A tall figure stood at the open door. Carter was in his usual khakis and a short-sleeved collared shirt made out of airy white fabric, accepting a glass of water from her mother.

"Look who's here, baby!"

"Hey," Bryce said, the knot in her stomach dissolving.

"Hey," Carter echoed, taking a sip of water.

"To what do we owe the pleasure?" Bryce's mother called over her shoulder, heading to the kitchen.

"Just came over to say hi," Carter called, before adding more quietly to Bryce, "and to check on you, spaz-o."

"I'm fine," Bryce said, rolling her eyes. "You know I'm fine."

Bryce's mother breezed into the entryway, bearing a bowl of cold, lime-green gazpacho that probably looked better than it tasted. She handed it to Carter with a spoon. "Try this," she said. "So, do you need Bryce to come in for another scan?"

"Dr. Warren probably does need her, yes," Carter said, swallowing a spoonful.

Bryce shot him a death stare.

Carter mouthed *sorry* and cleared his throat, looking at her mother. "Is there lemon zest in here?"

Just then, the Grahams' door creaked open once again, peppered with knocks from Gabby's manicured hand. She popped in wearing a yellow halter dress and white espadrilles, her hair twirled into a messy bun.

"Helloooo . . ." she called, the door clicking shut behind her.

While Gabby and her mother exchanged tight hugs and compliments, Bryce moved behind Carter. Her mother hadn't seen Greg or Gabby since Christmas break two years ago, Bryce had gathered. Gabby was the one who had taken that picture of her family with the wreath outside of Vanderbilt Medical. Had Greg and Gabby already been dating when Gabby took that photo? Probably. Bryce dug her teeth into her lip and smoothed her hair, bracing herself for Greg's entrance.

But the door stayed resolutely shut. Bryce felt a mixture of disappointment and relief. She cleared her throat. "Greg's not coming?" she dropped casually.

"Oh, no, he's here," Gabby replied with a wave of her hand. "He's just waiting in the car."

Carter was now balancing the bowl on the palm of his hand, untouched after the first sip. Gabby smiled deviously. "And this is Carter, right?"

"Yeah . . ." Bryce began.

"Carter," Gabby said, giving his shoulders a squeeze. "Come with us!"

"Nah . . ." Bryce said, answering for him.

"Yes!" Bryce's mother clapped her hands. She looked visibly relieved at the suggestion.

Carter looked at Bryce. She shook her head subtly. "Don't you have homework to do?"

"I always have homework," Carter said with a shrug.

"Let's go, you two," Gabby grabbed each of them by the hand, dragging them out the door. "See you later, Mrs. Graham!" she called.

Bryce allowed herself to be drawn toward the car, where Greg was sitting sullenly with the door open, wearing a white Hanes T-shirt and his old, worn Adidas flip-flops. At the sight of Bryce, his face lifted into a broad smile. He gave a short wave. Then he noticed Carter, and his eyes narrowed.

"Double date!" Gabby called, slipping into the driver's seat.

Carter and Bryce exchanged looks as they settled into the backseat. "Carter is a *friend* of mine from the hospital," Bryce clarified. Greg's eyes lingered on hers in the rearview mirror, asking the silent question he had no right to ask.

✻

Technically, the VFW was a community center for veterans of foreign wars. It was also the cheapest place to go bowling in Nashville. And, as many of the kids at Hilwood knew, the best place to drink when you were underage. The grizzled Vietnam vet who ran the bar didn't ID anyone who looked older than thirteen, as long as they listened to him talk about his time stationed in Saigon. The classic rock blared. Bowling balls crashed down the lanes launched by pot-bellied bowlers. Large fans on either side of the room hummed.

As the bartender filled a pitcher full of foamy beer, humming "We Are the Champions" along to the tinny speakers, Greg brought over old bowling shoes.

Bryce reached out for a pair. Greg lifted them out of her

grasp. She tried again, and again Greg pulled them away. Bryce couldn't help giggling. Greg was smiling, watching her struggle.

Carter banged his hand on the bar's surface. "Well," he said, "I'm going to get my own shoes."

Gabby pulled Greg to accompany her on her turn, where he stood behind her and guided her arm to the proper trajectory. Bryce looked at them and found it hard to concentrate on anything else.

She pretended to tie her shoes. She untied and tied the knot three times.

"So how do neurologists do, generally speaking?" she heard Gabby say above her. They had returned to the orange-and-brown plastic seats.

"We work on commission," Carter said dryly. "The bigger the brain, the bigger the paycheck."

Bryce felt him looking at her. She sat up and laughed too late.

"So, Bryce, your brain—" Carter pretended to speculate. "Probably, close to one hundred K in total."

"That much, huh?" Greg said, looking at Carter. His face was blank.

"Oh, yeah." Carter reached over to put his hands around Bryce's head. Bryce snorted and lifted her shoulders at his touch. "Bryce has a *big* brain. I've seen it." He gave her head a little shake.

"Gross," Bryce laughed.

"Have either of you ever eaten brain?" Gabby leaned in. "It's delicious. Greg and I had it when we were in Spain, remember?"

Greg, who had lifted his arms into a stretch, let an arm fall on Gabby's shoulder like it was the most natural thing to do. Bryce looked at the table's crusty surface.

"Nah, it was in Morocco, remember?"

"That's right," Gabby said. "But first, we were in Spain, standing on these ruins. And these weren't the tourist ruins, these were ruins Greg and I had just *found*, because he gets these feelings sometimes. He just goes off . . ." Gabby put a cool hand on Bryce's forearm. "You know, Bryce. He just goes off sometimes, forgetting anyone else is there, and you either follow him, or you don't."

Greg's mouth twitched into a smile.

"Anyway, we were standing on these coastal ruins, and the wind was blowing off the water almost hard enough to knock us over, and Greg and I were just watching the Mediterranean crashing against the rocks, just staring out for a long time. It was the most raw feeling. It was like we could conquer the world."

Gabby took a sip of beer. "And he turns to me and says, *Gab, let's go to Morocco.* We'd both spent most of our graduation money by that point, but I had made friends with this fisherman on a pier over near the beach who was willing to take us for half the price. So that settled it. We just said, *Screw it. Let's go to Morocco.*"

Greg was shaking his head, happily lost in the memory. "I felt like we could have gone anywhere in the world that day."

"It sounds awesome," Bryce said quietly. She had left the bowling alley for a moment, listening to Gabby talk about traveling. Growing up, she'd never been in a rush to get away; she wanted to go cliff-diving, sure, but she never put much thought into it because she always figured she'd have time, or that diving competitions would take her around the world. Now she wasn't so sure.

"Yep, thank goodness we got that all out of our system." Gabby took another sip of beer. Bryce looked up. "Now begins my journey through the exciting world of humanitarian law."

"We can still travel on breaks and stuff," Greg said, typing his name into the clunky bowling score computer.

Gabby pursed her lips. "I don't know about that. Rent in D.C. is pretty high."

"Glad we're paying an arm and a leg for a box," Greg responded curtly.

"It's worth it," Gabby said, taken aback.

"For you, it is," Greg mumbled.

"Okay," Gabby said softly, and reached out to put one of Greg's strands of hair behind his ears. "We'll talk about this later."

Silence. Carter finally spoke up. "It's Bryce's turn."

Bryce got up slowly and twisted her waist back and forth, loosening up. She chose one of the lighter balls, lifting it gingerly to her chest. Hopefully her daily rowing would serve her well.

As she swung back, momentum did its job. A clean shot, all but three.

Greg's turn. He got a strike. Gabby kissed him long on the lips, holding his face.

Bryce pretended to go to the bathroom but really took a lap around the bowling alley. Sitting at the table across from the couple was like waiting for her scores at a diving meet and never, ever receiving them.

When she returned, Carter rubbed his hands together as he stood, feeling out for the right ball in the row. He chose a large green fifteen-pounder.

Carter was a little taller and lankier than Greg, but he controlled his limbs with surprising grace, shooting the ball straight down the center arrow, only veering suddenly at the end. Strike.

Gabby took her turn, grabbing whatever ball was closest

and dropping it on the lane like she was tossing dirty laundry in a hamper.

Bryce took her turn to hurl the ball down the lane like a shot-putter. Strike.

"Miraculous," Greg said as she sat down, taking a swig of his beer. He winked at Bryce, and her stomach flip-flopped.

"So miraculous," Carter imitated him goofily. Bryce didn't know whether to laugh or kick him under the table. He chugged his beer down to the bottom of the glass.

"Slow down, there, turbo," she said, watching the amber liquid disappear down his throat.

Carter responded by looking at Greg and burping. Then he poured himself another. In reply, Greg chugged the rest of his own beer and slammed down his glass.

Two games and two more pitchers of beer later, Greg had won one game, Carter the other, and now they were on the edge of their seats, silently sipping their beer, waiting for their bowling balls to be ejected down the chute. When they spotted them come down the line, both guys shot up like they'd been electrocuted.

Gabby rolled her eyes and announced a girls' bathroom break.

Greg locked eyes with Bryce, as Gabby took her hand

to pull her away. Gabby led her fiercely toward the bathroom door, giving her *that look.* Her eyes were wide, her head tilted suggestively, as in, *I know your secret.* Bryce's heart raced. She had been looking at Greg too much, she knew it.

Gabby closed the door of the dingy restroom and immediately began fixing her bun in the mirror. "So, tell me," she said, retwisting her thick dark hair.

"Tell you what?" Bryce asked, her muscles clenched.

"Don't play coy." Gabby smiled devilishly. "What's the deal with you and Carter?"

Oh. Bryce's whole body sighed with relief. She felt like lying down on the dirty tile and going to sleep. "Nothing, really. We're friends."

Gabby tightened her ponytail, raising her eyebrows. "Well, there should be something."

"What do you mean?" Bryce asked, leaning on the sink, catching Gabby's dark eyes in the mirror.

"He can't stop looking at you," Gabby said in high, singsong voice. "And he's a *doctor.*"

"Please. He's in medical school," Bryce corrected, scrunching her hair.

"Well, whatever, I'm saying you should totally go for it." She smiled at Bryce, her bun now perfectly in place. "We gotta get some love in your life. Something is missing, I can tell."

"Well, we did kiss," Bryce said coolly.

"What! Why didn't you tell me?"

Because it was on the same day I found out you were engaged to my boyfriend, Bryce thought, but instead she just shrugged.

"I knew it!" Gabby threw her hands up. She put her hands on Bryce's cheeks. "I knew there was something. I know you, Bryce. I can always tell with you."

Bryce removed Gabby's hands from her cheeks with a pained smile. When they returned to the smoky room, the boys stood up from the table.

"I won!" Greg called. Sweat was starting to dampen his T-shirt. His beer-glazed eyes sparkled.

Greg threw his arms around Bryce in a celebratory embrace, and she let herself for just one moment enjoy the comfort of that place, to go back under the bridge with the train rushing above them.

But the train had passed, and Greg's arms loosened as he moved away to walk with Gabby. Bryce put a hand to her chest, at the hole she felt when he was gone, almost as if the train had passed right through her.

CHAPTER SIXTEEN

The next weekend, Bryce folded clothes with her teeth digging into her lip. Though she hadn't gone to bed until after one, she was up at eight, humming "Hey Jude" in the shower. The water was boiling hot, just like she liked it. She coated her skin with Sydney's vanilla body cream. Her oatmeal was buttery, covered in blueberries and cinnamon, a taste of home to fortify her for the day ahead.

She had seen bachelorette parties in movies. The purpose was wild fun, she knew that. But underneath the wild fun was the fact running through everything, the fact that the bride needed this one last crazy night before she and her groom would be together forever. Greg and Gabby together forever.

She zipped her old AAU diving equipment bag, packing a few things for the weekend ahead. Her head hurt.

Bryce knew what was happening then. It didn't come slowly, but it came in levels, like someone was turning up the knobs as the back of her skull was placed on the burner of a stove. Frostbite grew under her fingernails and across her toes. This time, when she was tipped on her head like a rain stick, she felt relief.

Hard dirt under bare feet.

The mute echoes of a place half full of water. It was dark, night. When she reached out in front of her, there was nothing but blank space.

Her eyes adjusted. She confirmed the solidness of the edge on which she stood, and quickly, as the moon darted between clouds, the glint of water.

Then, as if it was what she intended to do all along, Bryce bent her legs. Toes pointed forward, hands crossed in front of her. *Nothing fancy,* she told herself, and sprung off.

Air held her, gentle and familiar like an old friend. She allowed the breeze to cradle her until the last minute, when she made herself an arrow. She pierced its center and broke the liquid line.

Bryce knew as she hit that water was lifting around her body in a circle of precious, clear pearls, but a diver never gets to see her own splash. It's too bad, Bryce thought as she went under.

She came to on the ground, the carpet digging spots in her knees and palms as her head moved slowly out of fire.

She never used to fall over after the visions before. And her fingers still felt a little numb. *Not now.* She shook her sleeping hands, trying to wake them up. She wiped at her face and found a light streak of blood coming from her nose.

She let the throbbing subside. A knock on the door. Her mother's voice. "Hi, sweetie."

Bryce stood and wiped at her face again. She opened the door to her mother, who gave her a small smile.

"Carter's upstairs; he wants to do a quick checkup before you go," she said.

Carter was waiting for her in the kitchen as she carried her bag up the stairs into the cloudy morning. He turned around from where he was rearranging the Grahams' spice rack by flavor combination.

When he finished taking her blood pressure, he picked a piece of lint off her cheek. Bryce blushed.

"You look a little peakish."

"You sound like you're from the Victorian era."

He looked at his clipboard for no reason, clicking the clip at the top. "I care about you," he said, a little too loudly.

"Well, thank you." She didn't know what else to say. His eyes darted around, then back to her. They were so gray this morning. Like the sky.

"I mean, I woke up this morning and I remembered you were going away for the weekend, and I got so disappointed."

Bryce couldn't help but smile. "I'm just going downtown with a bunch of girls. So don't worry, you're not missing anything." She squeezed his arm and began to turn away. It was time to get going.

He stopped her. "No, I mean I'll miss *you*."

Bryce met his gray eyes. No, silver. They were almost silver. His shoulders lifted under his T-shirt in a small shrug. He felt tall to her. Taller this morning. Bryce swallowed.

His lips pursed. "I got something for you."

Carter pulled out what looked like a little silk package. He unfolded it and handed it to Bryce.

"A sleep mask," she said, smiling. It was navy blue silk with a gray rose pattern.

"It keeps out the light," he explained. "It'll help you sleep. Help with headaches, if you get them."

Bryce fingered the mask. I doubt anything could help this weekend, she thought, but she said, "Thank you."

Bryce's phone vibrated in her palm. *Outside!* Gabby texted. Bryce took a deep breath.

"I have to go," she said.

"Okay," he said. His smile was small, quiet.

Bryce turned with some mixture of calm and relief. She slipped the mask into her bag. She walked as quickly as she could down the empty driveway, feeling her damp, freshly showered hair.

A white hotel van idled on the other side of the street. Bryce climbed in and was immediately enveloped in a soft, fragrant group hug. All she could see was a tangle of Gabby's midnight waves, a short afro with a green scarf, and straight strawberry-blond locks.

They broke apart.

"So this is *the* Bryce!" said the taller of the two girls, readjusting the scarf around her tight black curls. Her smile was sweet, and her brown, long lashed eyes oozed sympathy.

The strawberry blonde laughed at her friend's expression and extended a hand. Bryce took it and got a closer look at the girl. She had bright green eyes and freckles. "I'm Zen," she said, "And that's Mary."

Mary pulled Bryce into another hug. "Yes, I'm Mary. I'm so sorry, you must be so sick of this, but your story is just . . . miraculous."

Two more girls sat in the back row of the van—both brunettes, one with a bob, one with shoulder-length hair. They were just like Gabby. Pretty, enthusiastic, sweet. Bryce couldn't remember their names, even though they had just said them seconds ago.

As someone handed Bryce a cup of coffee, the van started down River Drive. Their conversations bounced around her. Bryce felt the coffee run on a hot path from her throat to her stomach.

From the front seat, Gabby filled Bryce in about Mary's soon-to-be gig as a middle school math teacher in Oregon. Then Zen, a dancer from Vermont, started in on college gossip. Bryce watched their conversation like a tennis match.

"Did you hear about Gillian and Fred? They moved to Columbus."

"Columbus? Christ."

"At least they're not holed up in a closet in Bushwick. Madison looks emaciated, but not in a good way. She's taking the starving New York artist thing way too seriously."

"Madison is this wannabe fame-whore from the drama department," one of the brunettes explained from the backseat. "You know the type. Acts like she's still in high school."

"Oh my god." Zen's face broke out in a devious smile.

"Wait a minute. Bryce, you have to tell us how Gabby was in *high school*."

"That's right." Mary cocked an eyebrow. "There's only one photo of her on Facebook from back then, and she looks like one of those girls who goes to Renaissance fairs."

"What? No way." Gabby put her hands over her face. "Let's not go back there."

Bryce shrugged. Why was she so embarrassed?

"She's a great diver," Bryce said. She froze, realizing she was using the present tense. "She was that girl who would talk to anyone, no matter who it was. The smelly kid; or Rebecca, the bitchiest, most popular girl at Hilwood; or the principal; anyone. She didn't care about what lunch table she sat at, or if her lab partner had just gotten out of juvie, or anything like that. She didn't look down on anyone."

"Wait, so Gabby wasn't Miss Popular?" Mary looked at Gabby with mock surprise.

Gabby was widening her eyes at Bryce from the front seat, her mouth pursed. Bryce looked apologetically at her, wondering what she'd said wrong.

They dropped the subject as Mary dove into stories of her month building houses in Mexico this summer. Mary was a good storyteller, and her bright eyes flashed as she talked. She made huge hand motions and had a booming, clear voice.

She'd spent most of her time down south helping to build a school in Oaxaca, perfecting her Spanish, checking out the scenery. The rest of her time, however, was spent in the best restaurants and tequila bars in Mexico City.

"I'm a sucker for good tequila," Mary confided to Bryce. "And let's just say this weekend we'll be sampling a well-aged bottle I was able to get over the border."

"I can't drink," Bryce said sadly.

"Oh. Well, water will do fine." Zen lifted her water bottle to Bryce. "A toast! To a wonderful addition to our group!"

Zen, Mary, and the brunettes in the backseat lifted their water bottles, and Bryce had no choice but to join them.

Gabby smiled at the rest of them, and raised her own. "To great friends," she modified.

"And to you, Gabs." Mary beamed. "To you, and to Greg, and to love."

CHAPTER SEVENTEEN

Dum-dee-dee-dum-dum-DUM!"

"TEQUILA!" the rest of the girls in the car finished. Even Bryce roused herself from her thoughts. The tune reminded her of the pep band at a Hilwood football game.

Gabby let out a whoop and threw up her long, tanned arms. Her brunette friends followed suit. Bryce now knew their names were Molly and Hannah, though she was still deliberating who was who as the van ride was ending. They were both in "marketing," they said.

"Tequila at ten a.m.?" Bryce raised her eyebrows. They

were pulling up to the enormous old Opryland Hotel, where they were being treated to a spa day.

Mary extracted a tall shiny bottle from her tote bag. "Bryce, darling, perhaps you've never heard of something called a Tequila Sunrise."

"Trust me, Mary won't be able to take off her clothes for the massage without it," Zen said, leaning toward Bryce. Then, in a mock whisper, "She's kind of a never-nude."

"I heard that!" Mary shrieked. "Am not!"

As a bellhop in an old-fashioned uniform unloaded their bags, the girls rode the elevator to the top floor of the hotel. Inside the adjoining suites, enormous windows surrounded lush rugs on polished tile. Marble-topped tables held vases of fresh flowers. Bryce stepped up to one of the wall-length windows, Nashville spreading out below her.

When she turned back around, most of the girls had stepped out of their clothes and into large, white fluffy towels. One of the brunettes was lining up delicate glasses, portioning orange juice in each of them.

"Oh." Bryce tucked her hair behind her ear. "Aren't we . . . um, going to the spa?"

Gabby came over and draped a towel around Bryce's shoulders. "No, dear," she said, untucking Bryce's hair. "The spa is coming to *us*!"

As Bryce stuffed her clothes in her bag, she came across the blue printed sleep mask, and smiled to herself, thinking of Carter's gray eyes and his too-loud voice. *I care about you,* he'd said.

But she was distracted when white-outfitted people arrived and began moving furniture around to set up massage tables. Next came a row of three enormous leather chairs attached to tubs of steaming water.

"For pedicures," Zen informed her as she set up a row of candles.

In a blur, the girls drew the shades, lit the candles, and gathered in the center of the room for a Tequila Sunrise toast (just orange juice for Bryce). Then they positioned themselves on the various relaxation mechanisms around the room.

From a massage table, Bryce flinched at the touch of a stranger's hands on her naked back. She listened to the voices in the dark discuss LSATs, charity work, *Vogue Italia,* long-distance relationships. She listened as they turned her best friend into Gabby Travers, lawyer extraordinaire. Bryce had always thought she and Gabby were alike, at least in the ways that mattered. But Gabby had turned into this beautiful, confident woman with stamps on her passport and graduate school plans, Bryce thought as she watched her feet soak in the bubbling water. And Bryce hadn't turned into anything.

*

At dinner in a private back room of the velvet-curtain-covered, chandelier-lit Opryland restaurant, Bryce ate breaded squid for an appetizer, filet mignon and mashed fingerling potatoes for an entrée, and rich chocolate cake for dessert in the smallest, savoring bites. Because it was delicious, yes, but also because she didn't feel pressure to talk when her mouth was full. She may not have anything interesting to say, but she could eat.

After their plates were cleared, Bryce stood up awkwardly, looking at Zen and Mary for encouragement. They nodded, clapping lightly with excitement. They had wanted her to contribute somehow to the weekend, so she did her best. With swirly hand motions and a curtsy, Bryce presented Gabby with the silver tiara from the flea market, and a shiny pink sash that read HERE COMES THE BRIDE.

Gabby squealed and wrapped her in a hug. "Oh my god, Bryce!"

As they hugged, it felt for just a moment that Bryce actually *was* Gabby's best friend. Someone who really did know her best because she had known her the longest, because she had helped Gabby feel good when no one else could. Someone who belonged there.

"Thank you," Gabby whispered. She let go and turned to the rest of the group, the tiara perched perfectly on her head. "I feel like a princess!" She poured everyone a tequila shot.

Zen and Mary tossed their shots back, twisted their faces, and looked at each other.

"It's time."

They left briefly, returning with a projector they had rented from the conference center at the hotel, and portable laptop speakers. Zen dimmed the private dining room's lights as the words GABBY GORDON + GREG TRAVERS appeared on the wall.

The first slide was their baby pictures side by side—Gabby in a pumpkin outfit, already with thick curly hair, and Greg wearing a sailor suit, looking cherubic with thin blond curls sprouting from his round head.

"We're going to project this at the reception. But we thought it would be fun to get a little sneak peek," Mary said.

"Plus there are some embarrassing-ass photos we can't show with your grandparents in the room," Zen quipped. The other girls tittered. "We couldn't let them go to waste."

The second slide showed Gabby, eight, in a pink polka-dot swimsuit, drinking out of a hose.

I was there that day, Bryce thought. My suit had watermelons on it.

Greg, still chubby in a sport coat and khakis, outside his first middle school dance.

Gabby, fourteen, hair down to her waist, competing in the Nashville spelling bee.

She got eleventh. Out on the word exacerbate.

Greg at fifteen in an AAU uniform, flexing his muscles.

The first tournament we all dove together. Fifteen and under. Heat was rising up on Bryce's forehead. The colors on the wall flashed bright.

"I can barely remember those days," Gabby said dreamily.

Bryce closed her eyes, and in a flash, she was there again. It was more than a memory; she was actually there, inside that day seven years ago. The smell of chlorine tingled her nose.

Sunbeams filtered through the mist above the pool, the team gathering on the bleachers for the group picture. She slipped her arm around Greg's waist, her thigh feeling the heat of his. As someone held a camera up before them, Bryce and Greg shared a glance. But Gabby had also sidled next to Greg, nestling her head comfortably on his shoulder.

She's happy, Bryce could tell, and at the snap of the camera, Bryce was no longer at the poolside, the smell of chlorine leaving her.

The frame flashed to another picture of the three of them, a more recent picture. Recent, at least, to Bryce.

Gabby and Greg were unsuited, and Bryce was giving her tense, camera-ready smile, her warm-up unzipped, the USA suit shining through. The day of the Trials. The day that changed it all.

Gabby looked at Bryce through the darkened room, tears dotting her eyes. *I'm sorry,* she seemed to say. Bryce looked back to the slide show, her jaw clenching.

Then it was just the two of them. Gabby Gordon + Greg Travers.

Caught in the middle of a conversation in the halls of Hilwood, their backpacks beside them.

In a tentative, posed embrace at senior prom.

Outside their Stanford dorm, pointing with silly faces up to a palm tree.

Gabby's hair cut short, her arm around a younger-looking Zen.

Greg, his hair long again, smiling cheesily, holding up a fraternity pledge pin.

Greg, a pot on his head, kissing Gabby wearing cat ears with a grin on her face.

Gabby and Greg facing one another with their eyes locked, not realizing the camera was on them.

A self-taken picture at the beach, Greg's sunburned face slightly cut out.

Greg in a suit, cradling Gabby, the hem of her formal gown dangling from his arms.

Greg on one knee in front of Gabby on a beach, the Mediterranean sparkling behind them, holding a ring.

Bryce had had enough. The slide show went on for several more minutes. She watched the distorted reflections in Gabby's wineglass.

When it finally ended they all stood, swaying in their tequila-soaked state, and filtered out of the restaurant.

"Good night, Nashville!" Mary yelled as they exited.

When Zen opened the heavy wooden door to their suite, they all jumped. A chorus of male voices came from inside.

The girls pushed their way into the room. Gabby gasped. The brunettes screeched. Six young men in suits of various shades of blue and gray stood in the tiled foyer with their arms around each another, swaying as they sang out of tune. Their ties were loose. Their hair was mussed. In the middle stood Greg, singing louder than anyone. Bryce watched him as he sang the Stanford fight song they all knew so well. To Bryce, it sounded like a song in an old movie, something she'd never heard.

The chorus drew out the last note as long as they could. Greg fell into a high five and a hug with the guy on his right, who almost looked like his identical twin. Peter, his older brother. Bryce didn't know him well; he'd already been off at college when they were in high school. The rest of the guys stumbled into hugs with Zen, Mary, and the brunettes, shouting reunion greetings.

"What are you guys *doing* here?" Gabby finally managed

to get out among more, louder renditions of the Stanford fight song.

"We're crashing the party!" Peter threw up his long arms, landing them around Gabby's shoulders.

A tall, broad-shouldered guy with tousled red-brown hair swiped Gabby's antique tiara and put it on his head.

"Hey!" Gabby attempted a scolding tone, stomping her sequined heels. But Bryce could tell she was pleased. "This was supposed to be a girls-only night!"

"Aw, boo, Gab," said another guy in a pin-striped suit, his skin a shade darker than Mary's. "Don't kick us out!"

"Greg made us come." Peter pointed accusingly. Then he rolled his eyes. "He said he *had* to see his girl."

Bryce followed Peter's gaze. Greg was unbuttoning the top button of his dress shirt, shrugging. She forced herself to look away from his chest. He glanced up. "How could I be apart from this beautiful lady, even for one night?"

"Awww!" Gabby squealed. She marched over to Greg and planted a kiss.

The bachelor and bachelorette parties made sounds of disgust and delight, respectively. Bryce swallowed, feeling warmth roll from inside of her to the tips of her fingers. They had all missed one very important detail.

When Greg spoke, he was looking at her.

CHAPTER EIGHTEEN

There should be an Olympic event for taking stairs in heels, swear to freaking God," Mary shouted in Bryce's ear.

Fact Number Four about drunk people: they tended to shout a lot. Mary was clutching Bryce as they ascended from the lowest level of White Light. The dance club hadn't really been thinking of its customers when installing the only set of bathrooms down a set of rainbow fiberglass steps.

On her seemingly millionth trip down the dangerous rainbow, Bryce concluded facts Number One, Number

Two, and Number Three were that drunk people couldn't stop going to the bathroom.

Bryce and Mary cleared the top step and staggered through the sea of guys and girls in the blue flashing lights, looking to Bryce like a writhing Abercrombie catalog come to life. Mary lifted her bangle-laden wrist and yelled at the bartender for another Manhattan. The brunettes were shimmying on either side of Peter, one wearing a flapper-style fringe dress, the other in a cloudy pink satin. Peter looked like he was enjoying himself. Zen was in green sparkles, glimmering like a mermaid under the colored lights.

Bryce scanned the crowd to find Gabby, and scowled. She was dancing against Greg, her lips parted and her eyes closed. Bryce would rather not look to see how Greg was finding Gabby's backside. Instead, she looked at her feet in red pumps. They looked miles and miles away. She had always been tall; in heels she *towered*. She hoped her legs weren't showing too much in the silvery, shimmery dress she'd borrowed from one of the brunettes. It was backless, and suddenly she felt too exposed.

"Are you the designated bathroom helper?" A male voice came from her side. She turned to find the shoulder of the tall, tousled-haired guy who had stolen Gabby's crown. He gave her a tight smile. "Because I hear the stairs are dangerous, and I need to go."

"Ha," Bryce said. "I'm off duty at the moment."

"What's your name?" He turned his back to the bar and leaned. He had taken off his coat and rolled up his sleeves.

"Bryce."

"Tom," he said. "I'd buy you a drink, but I noticed you're not imbibing." He held up a glass full of ice cubes soaking in a deep brown liquid.

"Not tonight," Bryce said after a pause. She didn't feel like talking about the coma right now. "I'm on a solids-only diet."

An amused look crossed his face. "You're funny," he said, leaning closer to her.

"Easy crowd," Bryce said, backing away. She could smell the liquor on his breath.

She stole a glance at Greg. He was holding up Gabby's arm for a ballroom spin, but his gaze was in their direction.

"So what's next for you?" Tom asked, draining his glass.

Bryce lifted her shoulders. She was sick of this question. "I don't know."

"I mean, I assume you're a graduate."

"Nope," Bryce said, allowing herself a proud grin. "Not even high school."

It was Tom's turn to be confused. "So, you're a drifter. Just a wandering soul, taking in the world." He lifted his hand in an arc for effect. Before Bryce could respond, he said, "That's hot."

Bryce burst out laughing. She had just been called an attractive hobo. Tom mistook her laughter for encouragement, and he held out his hand.

"Dance with me, Bryce."

"All right." She took it. "As long as you don't make me go to the bathroom with you."

She led him between the moving mannequins to the center of the floor, just feet from Greg and Gabby. Bryce held Tom's hands and shook her hips. She twisted her knees and dipped down low. She hadn't danced in a long time. Dancing required muscles. It required athletics. And like anything else athletic, Bryce wanted to do it right. So she channeled her best Beyoncé, and she didn't care who was watching.

Tom swayed from foot to foot, bobbing his head. She looked up at him and winked. Why not? He probably wasn't going to remember tonight, anyway.

Next thing she knew, bodies were brushing past her. Greg, followed by Gabby. Greg's face was contorted in anger. Gabby was pouting, looking over her shoulder at the dance floor.

"I need some air," Bryce heard him say.

"I don't!" Gabby cried happily. She twirled back onto the floor and began shimmying with Zen.

Bryce caught Greg's eyes. He motioned his head slightly toward the exit. She looked back at Tom, who was now heavily involved in reciting the lyrics to "Party Rockers." Back to Greg. He had moved farther away from the dance floor, and he was still looking at her.

"Be right back," Bryce called, and bounced her way through the crowd.

She followed Greg's back at a distance until they were outside the club, where he ducked into an alleyway. Bryce rounded the corner of the building.

It had rained while they were inside, and now the pavement sparkled with damp under the streetlights, and the air smelled clean. She approached his silhouette.

"Hey," she said.

He turned around sharply.

"What's up?"

Greg let out a bitter laugh, rubbing his forehead. "You were making me jealous in there. You can't be dancing with my friends."

"Yes, I can," Bryce said quietly.

"Well, at least wait until I can't see," he said with a sad smile.

"I should say the same to you," she said, her eyes drifting to a flower Gabby had put in his hair. "Why'd you even come tonight?"

To see you, she wanted him to say.

"I don't know." He ripped out the flower and tossed it aside.

"Pretty pointless," Bryce said. She looked sadly at the discarded flower. Good things were gone. Forever was here, separating them.

A true look of pain marred Greg's face. He beat his fist on a nearby dumpster, filling the alley with a deafening thump.

He crossed to Bryce and held her tightly. She buried her face in the space between his neck and solid shoulder, smelling his alcoholic sweat, sweet even now. She could feel him breathing, as if he were a part of her.

Where Bryce lay her head, his voice hummed through his skin. "I don't want to go through with the wedding." Bryce looked up and wiped her eyes on the back of her hand. Greg held her by the shoulders. He stared at a spot on the damp cement, then back at her. "I want to be with you."

Her body sparked at his touch, hope welling in her. She saw them holding hands, riding in the front seat of his truck, going somewhere with nothing in particular to do, but always finding plenty to do. They would do everything together.

His face was growing joyous in front of her, so handsome in the alley light. "It's you, Bry. It's always been you."

But the weight of the truth was still there, underneath

it all, and Bryce recalled the bright images projected on the dark restaurant wall earlier that night—Gabby and Greg carefree with their faces pressed together at the beach, their sweetly awkward prom photo, Greg on his knees in front of Gabby with a look on his face that couldn't have been more sure. Each photograph, each moment in time, more proof that it *hadn't* always been Bryce.

She recalled the one and only time she went to Catholic church with Gabby's family, when she was a little girl. She understood the words, but she didn't know what they were *saying.* She had stared up at the stained glass, watching colored light angle through the etched people in robes. As Gabby and her family stood up and filtered out of the pews toward the front of the church, Bryce blindly followed Gabby's back. She saw an enormous figure in white, the parish priest towering over everyone, giving out crackers and little cups of red juice to each person in turn. When her turn came, she held out her hands.

But nothing came. The priest looked around, muttering something. People in line behind her looked over shoulders, impatient.

Gabby appeared, braided head lowered with embarrassment, ushering Bryce back to her seat by her shoulders while every face in the pews turned in disapproval.

"That was Jesus's communion," Gabby had explained in a solemn whisper. "You aren't ready for that."

So that was it. Once again she was the awkward little girl, pushing into the line for crackers and juice, blindly holding her hands out for a piece of something that was completely beyond her.

But this time there was no guiding hand to bring her back to her place. Somehow she would have to usher herself out, back down the aisle, back to where she belonged.

Bryce unhooked his arms from around her. "You loved Gabby for almost five years, Greg," she said, forcing the words out. "I think you still love her now."

Greg put a hand up to his sweaty hair. "That was a mistake. This is all a mistake. . . ."

Bryce shook her head, backing away. She didn't know how much longer she could stay out here, alone with him, saying the things that neither of them wanted to hear.

He held out his hands, searching her face. "I'm asking *you*, Bryce, to be with me. Are you saying no?"

Bryce closed her eyes tight against the sight of him, her first love, trying to keep back the tears. They were coming out anyway, falling from her lashes. She couldn't bring herself to say that word, *no*. Because saying *no* meant saying *yes* to a whole lot of nothing.

The loneliness she'd felt the day she found out Greg and Gabby were engaged began to line her insides like steel. She wasn't just losing Greg, she was losing *Bryce and Greg*. She was losing the part of herself that had belonged to him, and she had no idea what kind of person was left. She had already lost Bryce the diver. Now she was failing at Bryce the sister and daughter, Bryce the friend. She had woken up, and the time that had passed was like a wall between her now and her then, keeping her out, holding her back.

Who was Bryce when they had all left her behind? She was scared to find out. But she knew that she needed to.

"I'm saying you should marry Gabby," she said. "And leave me out of it."

When Bryce turned and walked away from him, she knew it would be for the last time.

CHAPTER NINETEEN

The rest of the night was in slow motion. Bryce floated among the jumping bodies in real time, their glinting jewelry and ice-filled glasses making her vision glow at the edges. She felt the silvery fabric of her dress against her skin, sending waves of cold to her bones. The hip-hop blasting from the speakers might as well have been a swelling orchestra, or a tinkling piano playing to an empty room.

Greg joined the mass of his friends, leaping in time to the music, taking shot after shot until he could barely stand.

In every interaction, she was half there. Half listening to

Tom tell her about the time he almost broke some guy's neck when he played football for Stanford. Half holding Zen's hair back as she upset the contents of her stomach in the toilet. Half dancing with Gabby when she dragged Bryce onto the floor.

The other part of her was still outside with her heart stopped. She had done the right thing, but no good feeling came. Nothing came. Emptiness was all.

Her two halves came together with a snap when she heard Gabby's voice. "I'm ready to go," she said, taking off her heels, her eyes half closed. "Let's go back to the hotel."

The parties exited in a herd of arms wrapped around shoulders, bare feet, shoes dangling from hands, and even some sloppy kisses.

Inside their suite, Bryce took a long time washing up. She would run the faucet, stop and stare at nothing, forget what she was doing. By the time she entered the bedroom, three lithe, still-dressed bodies were sprawled on the king-sized bed, fast asleep. Zen was asleep on the couch. Bryce tiptoed to each one, removed their shoes, and stretched out on the down comforter of the second bed.

But Gabby was still up. Bryce could hear her filling a glass of water, through a crack in the bathroom door. When Gabby emerged, she gave a heavy sigh and drifted out to the main room. Bryce looked at the ceiling, took a deep breath, and followed her to the far windows.

"Contemplating?" Bryce asked.

Gabby turned around, her eyes bright, still drunk. "Oh, good, it's you," she said, her voice thin and tired. She grabbed Bryce's arm. "Come with me!"

"Where?"

Gabby slid up the pane and stepped through the open window into the night air. "Come on!" she repeated, and with a dangerous sway to the left, she disappeared.

Bryce stepped through to climb the rickety fire escape behind Gabby's barefooted form. Of all places she thought she'd end up tonight, following a drunk Gabby up a fire escape was not one of them. But something about it was right in the rest of a terribly wrong evening. The stupidity of it, mostly. They could fall, but so what? Bryce was sick of doing the right thing all the time.

"Look, Bryce!" Gabby called down ecstatically. She was propelling herself over a wall at the top of the ladder. Bryce followed suit.

The roof of the Opryland Hotel was an expanse of bare cement except for the center, where thick steel girders held up an enormous neon sign. Bathed in the red light of the giant cursive, Bryce and Gabby caught their breath.

"I'm still totally plastered," Gabby breathed, laughing.

Bryce laughed with her. "I'm glad you're scaling the side of buildings, then."

They stood in silence for a moment, taking in the blur of lights below them.

"Are you having fun?" Gabby turned to Bryce.

"Yeah!" Bryce tried to sound as enthusiastic as possible. "Definitely."

"You're faking," Gabby said, with a scolding look. "I can tell."

"No, I'm not," Bryce said quietly.

"I'm having the most fun ever," Gabby said, and then, suddenly, her lip began to tremble. Tears rolled down her cheeks in black, mascara-filled streaks.

"Gab!" Bryce put her arm around Gabby's bony shoulders. "What's wrong?" Bryce glanced around the empty roof. She had no idea what to do. She had rarely seen Gabby lose control.

"I'm—I'm—sorry," Gabby sputtered. "It's just, it's really good to be home."

"It's really good to have you home."

"I felt like I could let loose," Gabby sniffed. "It was good."

At *good*, she collapsed in Bryce's arms, her chest heaving with sobs. Bryce tore her gaze from the cracked concrete. "What's *wrong*, Gab?"

"I just feel so much pressure," Gabby said between sobs. "With all these people in our hometown . . ." She swallowed another wave of tears. "They're all so perfect, they know what they want to do with their lives, and I'm just putting on a big show. . . ."

"Are you kidding me?" Bryce almost laughed, but she held it in. "You're going to one of the best law schools in the country!"

"Yeah, but I don't know if I can keep up," Gabby confessed, shaking her head.

"But when you first told me, at the restaurant, you didn't look like you weren't sure. You looked, like, ready to go."

"I was trying to impress you."

Bryce scoffed. "Impress *me*? The girl who couldn't walk?"

"I don't know," Gabby said wistfully. "I wanted you to think that I'd done so much while you were asleep. God knows you would have done more. Probably a gold medal by now, right? Maybe two?"

Gabby smiled through her tears, and Bryce laughed, softening. "You don't need to impress me."

"I hope I don't mess it up," Gabby said, burying her head into Bryce's arm, her dark hair fluttering in the breeze. "Law school is going to be so *hard*."

"Oh, stop." Bryce shook her head. "You're smart. You're

strong. You can do anything. And . . ." She gulped. "And you'll have Greg."

Gabby heaved a sad sigh. "I honestly don't know if he'll like D.C. We've been fighting about it, about Greg getting a job. But . . . I need him with me." Gabby leaned next to Bryce, putting her head affectionately on her shoulder. "I've lost so many people I love. I don't want to go it alone."

Bryce thought with a pang of the pictures she'd seen of Gabby's father—of his handsome, bearded face, his kind dark eyes. In a way, Gabby lost her mother that year, too. She was never the same after her husband died. And then there had been Bryce herself.

"Not all of them come back like you do," she added playfully.

Bryce wriggled out from Gabby's arms.

Not all of them come back. She couldn't argue with that. Her thoughts were too twisted, her mind too tired, her eyes too full of city lights, her disappointment too great.

So Bryce sighed, shaking her head at the world that didn't look nearly as cruel and confusing as it felt, and followed her best friend back down the ladder.

CHAPTER TWENTY

ryce stood in the doorway of her house. The van
honked as it pulled away. The party was over.

She tossed her house keys on the table by the
door, and saw a note in her mother's loopy handwriting:

Bry— off to Aunt Martha's until Sunday. Call us or
Carter if you need anything—said he'd be around. Love, Mom.

Bryce sat at the kitchen table, her bag at her feet.

Her hands were clenched in fists as she stared at the table.

She had brought all this on herself. Kissing Greg, wallowing in the past, letting herself hope for a different future . . . it had all been her fault. She felt helpless, but worse. Like she was sinking to the bottom of a pool with weights around her ankles, and she had strapped the weights on herself.

She looked at the clock. An hour had passed just sitting.

Every part of her was tense. She needed to not feel so much, to make everything less sharp and real. She needed to be numb.

Bryce entered Sydney's room. As usual, it smelled like her vanilla lotion, cigarette smoke, and a sweet, herbal smell Bryce didn't recognize. She dug through drawers, tossing clothes onto more clothes, shoving aside art pencils, scissors, hair bleach, scratched CDs. And then she found it. Alcohol. The scent wafting from the blue, half-empty bottle was unmistakable. TRIPLE DISTILLED VODKA, the label read. It wasn't tequila, but it would have to do.

Bryce grabbed a jug of orange juice from the refrigerator and made her way down the stairs, out the basement entrance. Her entrance.

"This is perfectly legal," she said to no one, stomping through the field full of dry grass.

Once in the barn, which looked even more ragged and dusty in the daylight, Bryce twisted the lid of the blue bottle and took a swig. Her throat was on fire, shooting flames down her chest to her stomach. When the bitterness on her tongue got so bad she began to gag, she remembered the orange juice.

She perched on a stray beam. She used to sit in this very spot, keeping her dad company while he worked on his plane. She took another swig. "To flying," she said, and laughed to herself. When she felt this wound up at seventeen, she just took dive after dive until she was so tired she couldn't think. But she couldn't do that anymore. She took another swig, "To Sydney," and something like hot molasses was traveling through her veins. Sydney was probably out drinking right now. Bryce doubted her sister would ever toast her, though.

She drank to the last night she spent here with Greg, to the shivering feeling that came when she was with him, like she would explode from happiness and fear.

She drank to Gabby, who had better have the best married life of all married people, ever.

The booze was working.

She climbed into the barn's loft and was pleased to see the rope she had tied to the rafters was still there. She loosened it, upsetting a roost of swallows. She poised her foot on the knot she tied when she was nine, tightening her legs and arms, ready to hold on. And then she was swinging, flying with the birds through the clouds of five years' dirt, silence except for the flutter of wings, the fibers from the rope pulling against the beams.

She made up a game where she balanced the blue bottle on a shelflike piece of wood protruding from the hayloft walls. She swung wildly on the rope, steering herself so that she could swipe the bottle off the shelf for a drink, and then set it back on her return trip.

But she got bored when she became too good at that game. She was too good at games.

She returned to the house, the bottle almost empty. She stopped at the pool. The ripples seemed to attract the sky's colors more than usual.

And then, without a thought, she crossed her hands in front of her, and dove in.

The water was cool and familiar. Her clothes weighed her down. She could have been swimming through pudding. But she managed a few laps. No freak-outs. No weird flashbacks. The water didn't morph or meld into anything other than what it was. Everything was free and easy.

Free and easy, Bryce thought. She turned over to float on her back. Dead man's float. She wondered if she was drifting, or if the clouds were drifting, or both.

*

Time had passed. She was being dragged out of the water. Her back scraped the edge of the pool. She struggled to her hands and knees on the patio.

A voice above her asked tensely, "What the hell are you doing, Bryce?"

Sydney. With difficulty, Bryce stood up to face her sister. Then she abruptly turned to go through the open doors, dripping water on the basement tile, and vomited into her hands.

Alarmed, Sydney followed her quickly, watching her retch. She ducked outside to the pool, and came back with the blue bottle. "Oh my god, Bryce. Are you drunk?"

Bryce froze, disgusted, holding back the next round of vomit. She was sobering quickly.

"Go take a shower," Sydney said, either trying to hold back laughter or vomit of her own. Bryce couldn't tell. "I'll take care of this."

"No, don't," Bryce said, wiping her hands on her shorts, trying to stop the ground from spinning.

"I'll take care of it," Sydney repeated.

Bryce had little choice. Her clothes felt almost too heavy to move. There was vomit in her hair.

She stood in the shower until her hair was rinsed clean. Then she sat down, her bare backside and thighs on the white porcelain tub, her legs crisscrossed, letting the hot jets hit the back of her head, her neck, sending a feeling of intense calm through her spine and all the rest of her. All the mistakes washed away, at least for the moment.

When she came out of her room, dressed in a new T-shirt and basketball shorts, it was evening. Sydney was gone. At least she seemed to be. She was usually gone by now.

Bryce was overcome by her sister's absence. By the emptiness of the house. What would she do, all alone here? What she normally did, she guessed. But what was that? For some reason, she couldn't remember.

"Bryce?" she heard Sydney's voice above her. "I'm upstairs!"

Bryce's anxiety melted away. She found Sydney lounging on the couch in front of the TV, wearing men's boxers and a tank top.

"You're not going out?" Bryce asked.

"Not tonight," Sydney responded, her eyes on the screen.

Bryce's first instinct was to ask if she could sit down. On her own couch. Next to her own sister.

"Nothing's on," Sydney said.

Bryce sat down. "That's okay."

"So," Sydney said, absently landing on a channel. A school of jellyfish appeared on the screen, part of some nature video. "What was that all about?"

Bryce sighed. The problems she had washed away were crawling back. "I messed up."

"You mean you *got* messed up?" Sydney turned to her with a wise smile. "Because that's what it looked like."

"Both." Bryce turned her gaze to the jellyfish. They glowed unnaturally on the screen, their white translucent skin dominating her vision.

"Tell me why," Sydney said.

Bryce didn't want to answer that. "I'm sorry I drank your vodka," she said instead.

"It's fine; just tell me why you drank it."

One jellyfish had broken off from the pack. Its tentacles jutted out to suffocate a sea star. Bryce became immersed in finding the sea star's flashing orange legs among the pink-white neon of the jellyfish. She had to fight the urge to follow it through the midnight water, reminding herself that it was just on screen.

She turned back to Sydney. Bryce could tell her sister, she decided. She had to get it all out somehow. "You promise you won't tell?"

Sydney made a noise for "Are you kidding me?"

"Okay," Bryce said. She took a deep breath. "I've been . . . seeing Greg. Behind Gabby's back." Bryce closed her eyes. She didn't want to see Sydney's reaction.

"Wow," she heard Sydney say. "Huh. I didn't think you had it in you."

Bryce opened her eyes. Sydney wasn't shocked or disgusted. Sydney was facing her, her head resting on her hand, looking steadily at her sister. She wasn't wearing eyeliner. She looked younger. Softer. More like the old Sydney.

She sat up. "Yeah . . ." Bryce said. "Me neither."

"So what are you going to do about it?" her sister asked.

Bryce clenched her teeth, images from last night running through her head. She flashed to the anguished look on Greg's face as she walked away from him. "I already broke it off."

Sydney shrugged. "So, great. What are you torn up about? Do you still love him?"

She pressed her palms into her eyes. "I do. And he loves me. He wanted to go away together, but I said no."

Sydney stayed quiet.

"Part of me thinks since I already screwed up, I should just go all the way. Just take him back from Gabby and get my way, and everyone else be damned."

"You really think you could do that?" Sydney said with a half smile.

"I don't know." Bryce shrugged, even though she knew the answer was no. "How do you do it?"

"Do what?"

"Do what you want, and not care about what anybody else wants, or thinks?"

"Thanks a lot, Bryce." Sydney's voice was suddenly cold.

"Fine." Bryce scooted to fully face her sister. "What is your deal, anyway? What is the deal with you?"

For the first time she'd seen since Bryce woke up, Sydney looked hurt. "What do you mean, *my deal?*"

Bryce softened. "I don't know." She took a breath. "Syd, what happened between then and now?"

Sydney's mouth tightened. "First of all, I'm not as bad as you think. You judge me, you get pissy every time you see me just because I look different than you, or because I go out, or whatever. But you didn't even give me a chance. You need to loosen up."

Bryce shook her head. "You need to remember you have a family."

"*You* need to understand that you were literally dead to the world, and everyone thought you were going to be dead forever."

Bryce opened her mouth to respond, but something in Sydney's voice made her stop. The bite was gone behind it.

Sydney continued. "I was so young, and I just . . . didn't know how to deal. You were gone, and Mom and Dad . . ."

As Bryce began to understand, she felt a sharp pain in her chest, like a knife stuck in her. She thought of the vision she had seen, twelve-year-old Sydney crying quietly in the corner, with no one to hold her or wipe her tears. "They didn't know how to deal, either." Bryce's eyes clouded with tears. She wanted to comfort Sydney now, like she used to, to tell her everything would be okay. But she knew Sydney didn't need that anymore. She had grown up on her own.

Sydney just nodded. "It's like, when something that bad can happen, anything can happen, you know?" Her voice began to shake. "And if you're never sure if things are going to be okay, what's the point of anything being okay? What is 'okay,' anyway? Because I sure as hell don't know."

Bryce let out, "But you're more okay than I thought. And that's good." She looked at Sydney and touched her folded knee briefly. "You're really smart."

"Shut up," Sydney said, dismissing her.

"You are," Bryce shot back. "Smarter than me."

"No!" Sydney said, raising her voice. Then she smiled back serenely. "I know."

Bryce laughed, wiping her eyes on her sleeves.

"It's nice to see you . . ." *Like this,* Bryce wanted to say. "It's good to see you home."

"Yeah." Sydney rolled her eyes. "Got kind of burned out."

Bryce was silent. Burned out doing what? She wasn't sure if she wanted to know.

Sydney spoke up. "Listen, I don't know what really happened, but I think you're better off without Greg. None of us are the same as we were before your accident— not even you. If he's stuck on you, then he's stuck on the past you. You know what I mean?"

Sydney then grabbed the remote to unmute the TV. Bryce thought about what she had said. Was she really that different from the Bryce of five years ago? She guessed that it was hard to really see yourself, the same way divers could never see their own splash.

So who was she now? As she scooted closer to her sister on the couch, Bryce decided that it was time to find out.

CHAPTER TWENTY-ONE

Thunder rattled outside the tall windows of the library, spilling into the tap-tap of raindrops hitting the glass. Bryce drifted through the medical aisle, flipping through books full of the anatomy of the brain. Which part did dreams come from?

Were all her visions real?

Before the bachelorette party, she had seen herself dive. She didn't know if it was a memory or a premonition, but now she needed to know if she could really dive again. Did she have the ability to improve even more? She'd never be an Olympic athlete again—her body had already missed the point where it could have peaked—but she didn't want to be distracted by old goals. She wanted to make new ones. And it wasn't just about her body, either. She wanted to start everything again. It wasn't like before, when she wanted everything *back*. Bryce just wanted everything. Period.

Bryce remembered the first day she realized the visions she saw were real. The strange power she felt as she came to that conclusion. The hum that went through her body as she connected the Carter of her dreams to the one that stood before her.

Carter. She hadn't seen him since before the bachelorette party. It had only been a few days, but it seemed like forever. She looked at her phone. Nothing.

He'd always just been around. Sometimes she'd wanted him there, sometimes she hadn't. But today she wanted him. And she would have to do something about it.

She dialed his number, holding her breath after each ring.

"You've reached Carter Lynch. I'm unavailable at the moment, but please leave a message and I'll get back to you."

"Carter, it's Bryce."

She found herself smiling at the sound of his voice. The librarian gave her a stern look.

More quietly, she said, "I'm at the Vanderbilt Library. Do you want to come here? I figured you might be on campus somewhere. I mean, I don't just need a ride. I want to see you." Bryce paused. "I wanted to thank you for the gift, by the way. My phone is dying, so just come if you can. Bye."

She sat at one of the enormous oak tables and watched the light change through the stained-glass window. She watched the students walk around with their textbooks and messenger bags. She might have been one of them in another life. Maybe she still would someday. She'd have to do something with herself soon enough. She never liked school, but she liked reading.

Maybe she could become an English teacher, like Mr. Schefly, who she'd had junior year. When she had to miss class because of tournaments, he told her she didn't have to do the regular assignments. He told her she could write about diving instead. But she usually chose to do the assigned work. It wasn't that she didn't want to write, it was that she wanted to keep diving to herself. She feared that if she wrote about it, she'd be giving something away.

She watched the clock. Her phone had died.

She wandered through the shelves, looking for him.

It had been three hours, and he hadn't come.

She went outside, walking around the building, jumping at the sight of every tall, dark-haired guy. There were a lot of them, but not the one she was looking for.

Bryce sidled up to a pay phone, thinking she'd call home. As she put in the quarters and picked up the receiver, she heard, "Hey."

He was behind her.

She hung up the receiver, barn swallows flying in her stomach.

He walked up to her, his hands hooked on the straps of his backpack. "Hey."

"Hey." She pulled off her hood, feeling her hair wind up in coils in the moist air.

"You should really charge your cell phone," he said.

"I suppose." They stood in silence for a minute, looking at each other. "But isn't it more fun this way?"

"I suppose," Carter echoed her.

Bryce laughed. And when the laugh faded, she laughed again. Together, they walked to his car, standing much closer than they had to be.

CHAPTER TWENTY-TWO

Bryce sat in Carter's car with orchids in her lap, orchids to the right of her, orchids in the back. Such is the life of someone who knows a lot of people in the Vanderbilt Medical Center.

The past few days, Carter seemed to always be leaving her to go to the hospital. He had always done that, of course, but Bryce had never really thought about where he was when he wasn't with her. It got her thinking of all the people she knew there, the people she hadn't spoken to since she left.

One bouquet was for little Sam (but mostly for Vandalia, his nurse, who often mentioned in a loud voice how much she loved flowers), one was for Jane, who she hadn't seen since the CAT scan blowout, and the last one, the one in the back, was an apology to Dr. Warren.

Bryce was trying a new thing. Not just thinking good things, but doing them. So many people had helped her, and if she couldn't be a good girl who did whatever they said, the least she could do was say thank you for all they'd done. Now it was just a matter of convincing herself that setting foot back in the hospital was worth it.

"You ready?" Carter pushed a couple blossoms away from his cheek.

"No," she sighed, but she unhooked her seat belt and opened the creaky door.

They seemed to glide through the halls of the neurology wing, at least compared to the way she used to move through them. Jane was too busy to chat, but when Bryce handed her the flowers, she gave her one of those soft but strong hugs that Bryce loved.

Sam looked as peaceful as a painted angel, so Bryce left Carter to read him a couple of chapters of *The Adventures of Huckleberry Finn*, and headed toward Dr. Warren's office.

Dr. Warren was out, but the door was open. There was barely room to set down the orchids. Her desk was covered in pages and pages of type, pens and highlighters scattered across it. GRAHAM, BRYCE was at the top of every single sheet. Her heart beat faster.

She scooted a thick stack to the right and set the flowers down. *What, am I her only patient?* No way. Dr. Warren was the head of the department.

Bryce was curious. She picked up one the papers, an image of a brain. *My brain.* There were red circles around certain spots. Bryce could imagine Dr. Warren poring over her desk, scribbling notes on the scanned image, her normally stoic face twisted with worry.

She backed into a corner of the empty, daylit office. Something must be wrong.

But something was always wrong.

Her stupid brain. Things came out of it that constantly baffled her. Strange visions. Impossible sights. Crazy thoughts that made her do foolish things. She swallowed with a dry mouth and walked into the bright hallway to find Carter.

She could hear his voice coming through the doorway of Sam's room. He was speaking in a steady rhythm.

"'. . . she went on and told me all about the good place. She said all a body would have to do there was to go around all day long with a harp and sing, forever and ever. So I didn't think much of it. But I never said so. I asked her if she reckoned Tom Sawyer would go there, and she said not by a considerable sight. I was glad about that, because I wanted him and me to be together.'"

Bryce stepped inside. He looked up. "Hi," she whispered.

Carter smiled, and it took away the balled-up feeling in her stomach. "You don't have to whisper," he said.

"Sorry."

"Don't be sorry. You should just talk to him as if he was awake. I mean . . ." He stopped, getting a funny look on his face. "I never whispered to you. And look where you are now."

She understood. She remembered. She sat down in one of the patterned hospital chairs next to Sam. "Hey, Sam. Are you liking *Huck Finn*?"

He would be thirteen by now if he woke up, but he looked young, like a little-boy version of Carter. Handsome. Adolescence would have been kind to him. His face was light, unbothered.

"I loved it when I read it for English class. There are supposed to be all these metaphors in it, about politics and stuff. But I just liked it for what it was."

"That's strange," Carter muttered. "His heart rate's going up."

Bryce could hear it, too. The beeps went from slow and sleepy to a jumping quick. Bryce looked closer at Sam. His eyelids twitched. Her heartbeat began to match his. Heat shot from her spine into icy-hot streams of pain, but she gripped her chair. She couldn't feel her hands or feet, but she would not fall over; she knew she was seeing something else.

A riverbank.

Rushing water, two boys in handmade overalls running ragged through the trees in the humid summer air. It was vaguely familiar, but immediately Bryce knew this dream wasn't hers. Why was she there?

The boys yelled to each other in honey-dripping drawls, the sound cutting in and out like a shortwave radio, something about running from bandits, making an escape on the river.

She smiled at their game. She used to play games like that.

Then she realized, these weren't her dreams—they were Sam's dreams. His mischief-making, Huck Finn dreams. The boys tripped to a stop and tumbled down the bank. Their faces turned back up toward Bryce, red-cheeked and beaming and out of breath—the faces belonged to Sam and Carter.

The room returned. Bryce's heart and head were pounding in pain. Her forehead was beaded with sweat. She felt the blood flow back into her limbs, reviving them.

Carter was looking at his sleeping brother and seeing

nothing else, the book open in his hands. Whatever would happen to Sam, Carter was making it better. He was taking Sam on adventures. Tears pricked her eyes.

When they were out of the hospital, the automatic doors barely whisked closed, Bryce wrapped her arms around Carter. And then she lifted her chin up and kissed him, hard.

CHAPTER TWENTY-THREE

Bryce woke up, and the whole room was full of sunshine. Her clothes from last night lay wrinkled, half off, twisted in the sheets. It was far past morning, probably high noon. Carter's long-sleeve Vanderbilt University shirt was falling around her like a blanket. She brought a cotton sleeve to her face. It smelled like his Old Spice, and the richer, outside smells—sweat, grass, dirt.

For every day of the exactly fourteen days since she had kissed him, Carter had met her on the curb in front of the Grahams' big blue house and taken her out to lunch. Bryce knew it had been fourteen days, because each day they had gone to a different restaurant in Nashville. Mexican, fast food, Vietnamese, and even one little place that specialized in different kinds of noodles. The third day in a row he asked her to lunch, Bryce had asked if they were going to do this every day.

"We date now, right?" Carter had asked, wiping hot sauce from his mouth.

"Right," Bryce said quickly, feeling her face flush.

"This is what dating people do. They go on dates." He pulled out the pen behind his ear and began calculating the tip.

"Plus I've already been to all these places alone, and I want to show the employees that I have a girlfriend. Hear that, Tony?" Carter turned his head to call toward the kitchen. "I have a girlfriend!"

They heard Tony respond, "How much did you pay her?"

Girlfriend. Bryce shivered with pleasure at the word. It had been a while since she had felt like a girlfriend. And because she hadn't looked back once, hadn't even spoken Greg's name since her conversation with Sydney, *girlfriend* now had a whole new definition. She wasn't just a girl who rode around in Carter's car. They weren't Bryce and Carter. When they met people Carter knew around Nashville, he didn't introduce her as Bryce Graham, the diver, or Bryce Graham, the miracle girl from Vanderbilt Medical, or even Bryce, his girlfriend. Besides the day when he had yelled at Tony, Carter usually left that part up to her.

She gave each of his friends a strong handshake. "I'm Bryce," she would say. And that was that.

Bryce, a twenty-two-year-old girl who liked to lay in the sun in places where the sound of cars disappeared, who knew every single one of John Wayne's lines in *The Searchers*, and who could play a mean game of pretty much anything.

When they ran into people Bryce knew, she showed Carter the same respect. Not her boyfriend, her doctor, her anything. Carter was a dedicated student, brother, food-taster, and an avid organizer of pretty much anything.

Bryce and Carter just happened to like accompanying one another to lunch, and dinner if he had time between summer school classes, and to Bryce's backyard with a rapidly melting pint of ice cream, like they had done last night.

Bryce's cell phone buzzed twice on the bedside table.

One text was from Gabby, letting her know she and Mary and Zen needed help deciding what shoes to pair with the bridesmaid dresses. Bryce texted back, saying she would give Gabby a call later. Bryce scrolled to the second text. It was from Carter.

wake up we have business

She smiled and wriggled into a stretch. *I'm up I'm up*, she typed.

Yesterday they drove way out of the city, past her house, past streets that had names, to dirt roads, through fences around land that belonged to no one. They tramped through weeds, and he helped her up onto branches she could have climbed before, lifting her up.

She read his textbooks aloud to him while he paced around, climbing on rocks and the remains of old walls. She could barely pronounce any of the diseases or body parts in the books, but at least they could pretend he was studying.

Bryce had spent an hour that way, calling multiple syllable words down to him and listening to him define them, catching his eyes on her when she looked up from the book and feeling her face turn red.

"Isn't this boring for you?" Carter had asked.

"No," she said, because it wasn't for some reason. She liked to watch him think.

He stood on a mound of old rocks, his hand absent-mindedly on his lips as he conjured the right words, his long, lean muscles running from one angle to the other in the most natural way, unlike Greg, who sculpted himself at the gym with self-conscious purpose. Carter looked like he belonged out here, like he belonged everywhere.

She did everything around him without worrying, without having to think about who she was hurting, without remembering every little thing from when she was seventeen.

Her phone buzzed again. Bryce rolled like a log over to the bedside table.

k. you have pancake stuff?

"Mom!" Bryce shouted upstairs.

"What?" she shouted back.

"Do we have the ingredients for pancakes?"

After a while her mother called, "Sure." Then, "Why?"

"Carter can come over, right?"

When Bryce finally made it up the stairs—after a lot of sitting on her bed with no pants on, listening to the Beatles—she found Carter already explaining to her mom the science of pancakes that were fluffy on the inside and crispy on the outside. Sunshine hit the panes of the kitchen windows, leaving patches of warm light on the dark marble countertops.

Bryce's mom smiled at her. Bryce grinned back.

Carter stopped talking briefly when he saw Bryce. She was still wearing his shirt, and had managed to put on pants.

"Um," he said, looking at her. "Sorry, I lost my train of thought."

"You were talking about how to make pancakes," Bryce said, her eyes locked on his.

"Yeah." He shook his head, turning back to her mother. "So . . ."

She saw he still had ink stains on his fingertips from taking notes with his ballpoint pen. He noticed her gaze and smiled, casting his blue-gray eyes downward. He had been in her kitchen before, but not like this. Not after she had had her lips on his.

"You ready to start, then?" he said, rubbing his hands together.

She smiled at Carter. "Hang on," Bryce put a hand on her mother's arm. "Is Dad here? He loves pancakes."

"You're right," said Bryce's mom. "He usually goes on a walk now, but—"

"See if you can catch him!" Bryce said hurriedly. Her mother bustled out of the room.

When she disappeared, Bryce hoisted herself to sit on top of the counter, inches away from Carter.

"Hi," Bryce said. They were at eye level.

"Hello," he said. He lifted his hand to brush away a strand of her hair.

"I didn't know you knew so much about food," she said.

They heard the footsteps of Bryce's parents returning.

". . . and I was just thinking," Bryce's mother was saying as they entered. "It's been a while since I made them."

"Well, thank you, Beth." Bryce's father looked at her mother, his tone light.

Bryce's mother looked back at him. Bryce saw her pale pink lipstick turn up at the corners. "You're very welcome."

He sat down and spread out the *New York Times* in front of him as Bryce's mother warmed up the griddle. She pulled out frilly aprons for herself and Bryce. Bryce was pleased to see hers wasn't the one with the puffy rooster on the front. She hadn't seen these aprons since she woke up.

"Want an apron?" her mom teased Carter.

Carter glanced at Bryce's dad and said in a gruff voice, "No, thank you."

Bryce and her mother giggled.

Carter threw himself around their modern tile with the same furrowed brow he got when taking Bryce's blood pressure. He whipped pancake batter with precise strokes. He wiped his brow with one of their pristine white dish towels.

Things are better, Bryce couldn't help thinking as she watched the batter fall into perfect circles. Her mom had started going for long walks in the morning with ladies from the neighborhood before she immersed herself in her work. Her dad had come home from Vanderbilt and gone straight out to the barn until nightfall, returning to the house with his toolbox and not even bothering to turn on the TV.

Sydney shuffled in at one point in long underwear and an oversized T-shirt that said OBEY.

She stood near the stove and stared openly at Carter. "Why is the hospital guy in our kitchen?" Sydney looked at Bryce, and then said, "Oh."

"What?" Bryce asked. Was she blushing?

"You want to slice up some fruit?" Carter asked, and slid Sydney a bowl full of peaches. Bryce was about to make an excuse for Sydney, who usually only came down to get water, but Sydney just took the bowl and put it under running water.

"Sure," she said. Bryce's dad folded his newspaper over to look at his youngest daughter. Her mom looked up from the bacon in surprise.

"I like handling knives," Sydney said to no one in particular, and turned back to slicing peaches with a quiet fury.

Twenty minutes later, Carter stood there, brooding, as the Grahams loaded their plates. "They *taste* like they could use a pinch of salt, but I can't believe that. I measured it perfectly."

Bryce's dad snorted as he sat down on one of the high-backed chairs. "So sprinkle salt on 'em, what's the big deal?"

"The recipe doesn't call for more," Carter countered, taking a seat next to Bryce.

Bryce's dad reached for the salt in slow motion. Carter pursed his lips. Her dad tried to hold back laughter as he slowly tipped the salt toward Carter's plate, raising his eyebrows as if bracing for an explosion. Carter took in a breath. The salt fell. The rest of the table burst into laughter, even Carter.

Bryce dug into her pancakes whole, not bothering to cut them into small pieces like her mom always told her to do. Just like she remembered, her dad rolled his pancake up and dipped it directly into the maple syrup.

"You know what?" Bryce said suddenly, realizing. "I haven't had pancakes since I woke up."

"Maybe that's because you girls are never up before noon," Bryce's mom said pointedly, slicing her pancakes into little squares.

"It is possible to make pancakes after noon, Mom," Sydney intoned. She looked at Bryce. "The fund-raiser last year at Hilwood was a pancake feed. The seniors put it together. The pancakes were kind of gross, though. And then they also had a bouncy castle, which was a bad, bad combination. . . ."

Bryce let out a puzzled laugh. The rest of the table looked

at her. "I was just thinking how absurd it is that I literally slept through my senior year." Sydney looked sorry she'd brought it up. "No, Syd, it really is funny. What if I was just too tired to go to school and I overslept? That's basically what happened."

Carter gave her an amused, thoughtful look. "You slept through a lot of things, then. For some reason it doesn't seem so bad when you look at it that way."

"Be grateful you slept through when I had braces," Sydney said dryly. "It was not pretty."

Bryce's father chuckled "You could even make a list."

Carter squeezed Bryce's knee under the table. She nudged him, trying to hold back a smile. She thought about the things she'd done since she woke up, the mental list she'd made more than a month ago. *Sun, clothes, exercise.* Bryce had done all right with those.

"I'm going to do that," she said suddenly. "Check off items until it's all done."

"I do love checking things off lists," Carter admitted.

Bryce giggled. "Yes, I know."

Bryce had spent so much time longing for what she'd lost. She'd never thought of actually getting any of it back. But why not?

Bryce's father cleared his throat. Carter and Bryce looked

at him and sat up straighter in their chairs. They had their heads pretty close together.

Her dad folded his arms. "I noticed that you were talking closely with your gentleman caller at my breakfast table."

Bryce braced herself for a lecture. Sometimes her dad got an old Southern streak in him.

"Gentleman caller?" Sydney asked with disbelief. "Really?"

He looked sternly at Carter. "Can the first item of said list be more pancakes?"

CHAPTER TWENTY-FOUR

The first on Bryce's list of things she'd missed was cheesy senior photos.

Bryce had always loved when the Hilwood yearbook came out. She and Gabby would lie on Gabby's bed and make fun of the kids whose pictures looked like glamour shots from the mall, or who had taken shots with their hands placed lovingly on their pickup trucks. Some kids took pictures with their dogs. Everyone's smile was forced, their turtlenecks or sweater vests picked out by their parents. The best part was that Bryce and Gabby and Greg were all supposed to have done the same thing. Bryce's had been scheduled for right after the Trials—so she could give a thumbs-up while wearing an Olympic T-shirt.

But this time around the photos would be even cheesier, Bryce decided. The cheesiest version of everyone's worst pictures.

"Are you sure?" Carter had asked as they checked out a nice camera from Vanderbilt's media department. "Don't you want to look back on these?"

"I'd be betraying my high school self if I took this seriously. Trust me," Bryce replied.

They went to Percy Lake, and Bryce basked on the rocks in her best clothes, holding her head at weird angles while Carter told her to look natural. They had already done the obligatory "wheat picture" that no Tennessee girl could do without, where Bryce stood in shoulder-high grasses in her letter jacket, pretending to push the yellow blades aside with a mystical look on her face.

The last one was of Bryce surrounded by her diving trophies. Every single trophy or medal they could dig out, they used. It turned out to be about thirty-five. Carter complained he could barely see Bryce behind all the trophies, yet there she was, putting her fist under her chin with a gigantic grin on her face.

The pictures had turned out cheesily excellent. Bryce had even asked Carter to Photoshop them to have a cloudy outline like the mall glamour shots, with the words *Bryce Forever* engraved in shiny letters in the corner.

The second item on the list was the homecoming football game.

Bryce loved football games. She loved being in the middle of the crowd. She loved how everyone in the stadium stood up when Hilwood was about to score a touchdown. She loved the pep band's terrible rendition of "YMCA," and that no one paid attention to the pep band in the first place.

"How are we going to do this in the summertime?" Carter asked as they sat on the walking bridge over Highway 12, swinging their legs. "Football doesn't start till September."

A truck carrying lumber zoomed underneath them. Bryce's popsicle dripped, hitting the pavement where the truck had just been. "Wait, what day is it?"

"Wednesday."

"The . . ."

"Twenty-second."

She stuck the remains of the popsicle in her teeth and stood up on the bridge. "Let's go!"

Bryce and Carter sat in the empty bleachers of the third practice of the Hilwood Raiders' season, wearing T-shirts with scowling cartoon pirates on them, sweating in the August heat. They cheered loudly whenever the team executed a drill correctly. They stood up whenever anyone got close to the end zone, including Coach Farmer, Bryce's old geography teacher.

When they decided it was "halftime," they drank cold Cokes, and Carter brought out his iPod speakers to play all the songs on *ESPN Jock Jams*. When "Hey!" came on—the song where everyone was supposed to shout "Hey!" every three notes—the assistant coach had to ask Bryce and Carter to leave, as they were a distraction to the team.

"'Bye, Coach Farmer!" Bryce called as they left the stadium. "Have a good practice, guys!"

The third item on the list was laundry, but it was a late addition. Bryce's mother had caught them on their way out one day, with Bryce's hamper in her hand.

"You seem to have missed learning how to do this, too," her mother had said.

The fourth item was graduation.

The morning she was going to pretend to graduate, Bryce felt oddly formal. She had to pull some strings at Hilwood by e-mailing Mr. Schefly, but they were able to get into the auditorium on Thursday morning. They swung by Gabby's house on the way, to borrow her cap and gown, and Carter had replicated Hilwood's diploma and printed it with Bryce's name in curly script.

He sat in the audience while Mr. Schefly stood at the

podium in his usual sweater-vest and combover. Bryce stood backstage in a short sundress under the gown, and her Converse. "Pomp and Circumstance" played from the tiny speakers Carter had hooked up to his iPod.

"Bryce Cornelia Graham," echoed through the auditorium. Bryce strode across the stage, gave Mr. Schefly a firm handshake, and waved at an imaginary crowd of classmates and family. She'd suggested to Carter that they get cardboard cutouts of everyone in the yearbook and put them in the seats, but Carter thought that would be overdoing it.

"Cornelia, huh?" Carter said after Mr. Schefly left.

"It's my mom's middle name, too," Bryce said, flopping on the seat next to him.

"Elizabeth Cornelia," Carter said thoughtfully, flipping open the diploma he'd made. Then he snapped it shut. "My mom's was . . . Carrie Ann, I believe."

Bryce felt her forehead tense. "Was?"

"Was." Carter said firmly. "She was in the car with my brother."

Bryce couldn't believe she'd never asked about it before.

"Wish she were still here," he said, gazing at the floor. "It'd be nice to have someone else to visit Sam besides me. Share the load." He looked up and smiled sadly at Bryce. "And she would have liked you."

"What about your dad?" Bryce asked.

"He thinks paying the bill is enough," Carter said, shaking his head.

Bryce had thought she knew loss. She had felt like her family had drifted. Like they had become strangers, irrevocably changed. But . . . Carter knew what it felt like to *really* lose his family. "Have you asked him to visit?" she asked tentatively.

Carter let out a bitter laugh, putting a leg up on the chair in front of him. "Come on. I shouldn't have to ask my own *dad* to visit his son."

"Everyone needs a wake-up call sometimes."

Carter looked up and gave her a winning smile. He put his hands around his mouth and gave a fake shout. "Ladies and gentlemen, your graduating class!"

On cue, Bryce threw up her cap. It landed a few rows away. Then she stood up abruptly, making her hinged seat bounce. "I want to do it for real."

"What, graduate?"

"Yeah," Bryce said, moving through the rows to retrieve Gabby's cap.

"You could probably do your senior year again, no problem," Carter said, following her.

"Ugh, I don't want to go back." Bryce had had enough of

the past. She wanted to move forward. "I want to graduate so I can go to college," she clarified. It was strange to say it aloud.

"I like that plan," Carter said. His tone became playful. "You have a bright future ahead of you, Bryce Cornelia Graham, Hilwood High graduate."

She threw off her gown and pushed open the doors to the Hilwood courtyard, feeling his eyes on her legs under her short dress.

When they got inside the Honda, Carter paused, looking at her. He reached over his seat to put a hand through her hair, and leaned his face into her lips.

"No distractions from the future!" she cried. He groaned, leaning back into the driver's seat. "To the bookstore for a GED prep book!"

Carter started the engine. Bryce scooted near him to tease him a little more, whispering throatily in his ear. "And then to the library to study it . . ."

"Who knew the future could be so sexy?" Carter muttered, smiling.

Bryce laughed and sat back in her seat. A comfortable silence settled between them. Bryce's thoughts drifted elsewhere as Carter turned up the Beatles singing "Ob-La-Di, Ob-La-Da" on the radio. She would find something she loved to study, like Carter had, and she would walk the steps every day to Vanderbilt's red brick buildings and listen to lectures. She would pore over books while she ate, and study all night for tests.

Bryce glanced over at Carter and unbuttoned the top button of his Oxford shirt. There was something else that came next, too. The more time she and Carter spent together, the more she thought about having sex with him. Or at least what she imagined sex would be like. She and Greg had never gotten that far. Another milestone Bryce had missed.

Carter glanced back at her and turned the music down, as if he wanted to say something.

"Yes?" Bryce said.

"I was just thinking . . ." Carter began, pondering. "*The Jetsons*."

"What?"

"The clothes they wear in *The Jetsons*. That's also kind of a sexy version of the future."

Bryce narrowed her eyes at Carter over a half smile. "Seriously?"

"What?" he said, shrugging. "Don't judge me. That was what I was thinking about. What were *you* thinking about?"

"Nothing," Bryce sighed, smiling broadly out the window. "Nothing at all."

CHAPTER TWENTY-FIVE

Bryce turned the camera on her parents. She selected the black-and-white feature from the photo options and told them to put their arms around each other. They rolled their eyes like two teenagers, but fell comfortably against one another, her father already in his gray sweatpanted pajamas, her mother still in jeans and a camel-hair blazer.

"No, like the picture!" Bryce said. "The one that used to be on the mantel."

"What was it—" Bryce's father adjusted his arm.

"We hold hands," her mom reminded.

They found the pose from their prom picture: the two of them in profile, facing each other, their hands awkwardly entwined in front of them. Elizabeth Gergich and Mike Graham had been high school sweethearts in their small town. She was a shy church girl. He was a star swimmer. They both grew up on farms. Bryce snapped the photo.

"Did you get it?" Bryce's mom left the pose to see the picture. She found the display. "Bryce, honey! You didn't have to do black-and-white. They had color photography back then."

"You guys look great," Bryce said, admiring her handiwork.

Her mother muttered, "My hair could use some volume, but that'll do. We don't need another one. What do you think, Mike?"

"You're the boss," he said.

"Bryce's turn again." Her mom hustled Bryce against the dark wooden door.

"No," Bryce said, adjusting her wrist corsage. "Wait for Carter."

Senior prom was the final item on her list because Carter had told her to save it for last.

"Get a dress and a corsage, leave the rest to me," he had said.

So there she was on a Saturday night, draped in a long, gold dress, her hair in a French twist, waiting for him like Christmas morning. Her parents had played their parts nicely. Her mom worried about the lily on her wrist matching Carter's tie, and asked for his phone number so she could know exactly where they were going and when they were getting home. Her dad tried to hide his wet eyes under the guise of "allergies" when he saw her come into the hall for the first time.

Finally, a knock sounded on the door.

Carter stood in her doorway in a fitted black suit with a thin black tie. He had combed a part in his dark hair. When he saw Bryce, he took a sharp breath through his nose.

"You are breathtaking," he said.

"So are you," Bryce said. "You look like a secret agent." It was true: he reminded her of a 1960s James Bond. Nothing got Bryce like men from old action movies. She bit her lip.

"Let him in, baby!" She heard her mother's voice behind her.

Bryce opened the door farther and Carter stepped in. *Snap!* The pictures began. He took his place next to her, putting an arm around her silky waist. *Snap.* Bryce took his boutonniere from the mantel and attached the lily to his lapel with its pearl-topped pin. *Snap.* Bryce had to stop herself from snatching the camera from her mother, but she supposed if she wanted this to be a real senior prom, then having her mom take way too many pictures was entirely necessary.

After what seemed like a lifetime of frozen smiles, Carter said, "Well, we should take our leave."

Bryce's mother put down the camera. "One. One a.m. sharp." She set her pale pink lips in a thin line. "I'm serious."

"Mom—"

"No, I'm trying to get better at this. I need to practice."

"Yes, Mother," Bryce said with mock obedience.

"That's better." She took Bryce and Carter in her arms. With Bryce in heels, her mother only came up to their shoulders. "Have a good time."

Bryce breathed a sigh of relief as they left the house, her heels clicking down the sidewalk. She took in the smooth night air and shivered with excitement. Carter's tiny old Honda hummed at the curb.

"I wish we had more luxurious transportation, but limos are surprisingly expensive."

Bryce smiled at the idea of her gown on the busted leather of Carter's seats. "It's perfect."

"But watch this," Carter said, holding her elbow. "Ahem!" He clapped twice.

A chubby guy in a rumpled button-down shirt came around the car, bowing slightly to Bryce.

"This is Jeffrey. He's in my anatomy class. He will be our driver for the evening."

Jeffrey straightened, then said out of the corner of his mouth, "You're still giving me fifty bucks, right?"

"Not in front of the lady, Jeffrey!" Carter said, winking at Bryce. "To the restaurant!"

Jeffrey rolled his eyes and opened the squeaky back door for the two of them. Carter had laid down a soft sheet over the patchy backseat, and in the center was a bucket full of ice surrounding a bottle of sparkling grape juice.

The Honda rolled forward. Carter had pinned up another sheet as a divider between them and the driver. He leaned over the bucket to give Bryce a soft kiss, just centimeters from her mouth, teasing her. "I don't want to ruin your lipstick," he said.

Bryce gave a small laugh, her eyelashes close enough that they brushed his cheek. She took in his handsome frame against the pinned-up sheets.

"Who cares?" she said, and their mouths connected. It felt like the last kiss in a romantic movie, but their night had just begun.

At the restaurant, Bryce tucked a napkin into the front of her strapless dress, and Carter ordered lobster for them to share.

"Special occasion?" the gum-chewing waitress asked with a twang.

"It's my senior prom," Bryce gushed loudly, and beamed at the other patrons, an elderly couple and a family with twins.

Carter disguised his laughter with a cough.

"Prom in August, huh?" the waitress said lazily, and then didn't ask any more about it. They all turned back to their meals.

After dinner, in the car, as Jeffrey ate their leftovers in the front, they popped open the bubbly. Carter dusted off two plastic champagne glasses he had put under the seat.

"To us," he said, topping the glasses with foamy white grape juice.

Bryce cleared her throat. She had thought of something to say at this moment, something better than the things she felt usually came out of her mouth.

She lifted her glass. "To a life worth reliving!" she said triumphantly, and Carter nodded.

They were holding their full glasses to their lips, ready to take a sip, when the car lurched forward, splashing fake champagne all over Bryce's dress and Carter's suit. They froze for a moment, taking in the damage.

"Sorry!" Jeffrey called back.

"Send back some napkins!"

Carter took a wad of napkins from Jeffrey's disembodied hand. Bryce's lap was soaked through and through. Carter started spreading the napkins on Bryce's upper thighs like picnic blankets, pressing them down to soak up the moisture.

Bryce started to giggle. "Could you stop pressing on my lady parts, please?"

Carter shot up, banging his head on the roof of the car. "Ow!"

Then they both started to laugh, Carter's eyes tearing up from hitting his head. He collapsed in her lap and she ran her hands through his gelled hair, messing it back into his usual bed head.

＊

They were acting out the scene from *Taxi Driver* Bryce had showed him in the hospital, trying to see whose de Niro impression was better, when Jeffrey pulled up to a row of buildings.

"This is it, right?" Jeffrey called back to Carter, his mouth full of dinner roll.

"This is it," Carter replied, and leaped around the car to open the door for Bryce.

Bryce stepped out into a street she didn't recognize. The buildings were a mixture of old storefronts and narrow houses with wide, white porches on both levels. She could see the skyline of downtown Nashville in the near distance. Carter led her to a door next to one of the old storefronts. It stood open under a humming neon sign reading THE JAZZ HOUSE. A few scattered beats from a drum set filtered down a set of wooden stairs.

"Welcome to your prom," Carter said, and took her hand.

She squeezed his hand tight as he climbed in front of her. Up the stairs a stooped old man in a beret sat on a stool. Carter placed a ten-dollar bill in his hand and led Bryce to a small table in sight of a group of unmanned instruments glowing in stage light against the rest of the dark little club. In front of the band was a semicircle dance floor.

The drummer lay down a few beats, bobbing his bald head to the rhythm. Bryce felt her mouth drop open in awe at his skill.

She looked at Carter, who smiled back at her, amused by her amazement. "They'll start in a few minutes."

One by one, the musicians took up their spots. A man with a big beard and gnarled hands at the piano, a tall woman all in black at the stand-up bass, a middle-aged man on trumpet. And finally the singer, a curvy girl not much older than Bryce in a tight, red dress, her hair styled in old-fashioned curls.

The first strains of music began, and Bryce felt her body melt. Carter had picked the exact right band. The notes didn't feel random like some jazz she'd heard; they came together in harmony and a familiar rhythm. The singer began, with a voice like warm maple syrup.

Hold me close and hold me fast

A couple moved to the dance floor, a woman in a sundress and her partner, a guy with dreadlocks. Carter looked at Bryce. They stood up together, moving around the table to find each other's hands. She wrapped her arms around his neck as he placed his hands on her waist. They swayed through the second verse.

I see la vie en rose.

"What's *la vie en rose?*" Bryce asked Carter.

"I think it's just 'life in pink,'" he replied, close to her ear. "The rosy life."

Bryce could feel everyone's eyes on the two of them in their formal clothes, but for the first time, she wasn't self-conscious. She knew she looked beautiful. Surrounded by these sounds, beside the candlelight flickering on the tables, everyone looked beautiful tonight.

She met Carter's eyes, which wrinkled at the corners as he smiled, looking her up and down. They drifted closer, and her head fell on his shoulder. She heard his voice near her ear again, his lips grazing her neck.

"I'm crazy about you," he whispered.

In reply, Bryce lifted her head, holding up a hand to the music. "Hear that?" she asked him.

When you press me to your heart
I feel a world apart
A world where roses bloom

"That," she said, and returned her head to rest on him.

They stayed that way until the song ended, and quite a long time after.

CHAPTER TWENTY-SIX

At Bryce's insistence, Carter parked on a side street, far from the center of downtown, so that they could have a nice, long walk to Gabby and Greg's rehearsal dinner.

"It's one of the last nights we can go outside before winter," Bryce joked as she took his arm. He had been silent the whole car ride over, and Bryce was trying to lighten the mood. Winter did come in Nashville, and sometimes there was even snow, but it was the opposite of winter this evening in early September. The humidity was almost unbearable. They might as well have been walking through a jungle.

"I guess so," he said, his eyes ahead.

Maybe he was tired. Today they had traipsed through the home section of Bloomingdale's, looking for Gabby's wedding gift. A skinny girl in a crocheted dress and huge glasses had scolded them for lying on the beds, and Bryce could have sworn she overcharged them for the oak tree–shaped bookends they finally picked off the registry.

Then Carter had to put in hours at the hospital. He showed up at her door looking dashing in loafers and a sport coat with reinforced elbows.

Bryce wore a dark blue, vintage-looking dress with a low neckline and a tapered waist, the skirt flaring out just above her knees. She was starting to recognize herself in the mirror, getting to know the shape of her curves and how to wear color. She liked who she saw in navy. It made her eyes stand out in fiery hazel. She had put up her waves in a loose bun on the top of her head, and slicked on some of Sydney's cinnamon lip gloss.

But Carter hardly looked at her.

Bryce looked at his profile. He had known her so long, and she was just starting to know him. But it was more than the start of something. So many days he had just sat next to her when she was asleep, when she was awake. He was steady, balancing her out, anchoring the other side of an always-tipping scale. She couldn't wait for the day when he needed her. She wanted to give back to him.

"Carter," she said, and stopped.

He took longer to stop walking, and turned around a few feet in front of Bryce. *I love you.* She could say it now. She should say it.

"Bryce," he said, his tone even. She wrapped her arms around him. "Bryce," he repeated, unhooking her arms, holding her hands.

"What?" she finally replied. She sniffed, trying to smile. Had things changed? They couldn't have. They were in love this afternoon, she knew they were.

"There's something I need to tell you." His jaw clenched.

Bryce pulled her hands from his. He let them go.

He crossed his arms, looking at the sidewalk. "This afternoon I sat down with Dr. Warren and reviewed what we were able to salvage from your CAT scan." He took a breath. "There were too many neurons firing at once, Bryce. Every time these neurons erupt simultaneously, there is damage to the brain."

"So?" she said petulantly. She felt childish, but she couldn't match the cold, flatness in his voice.

He cleared his throat. "The more damage the brain receives, the more it swells. The skull restricts the brain from expanding, and this leads to a rise in pressure within the brain. This rise in pressure quickly equals the arterial pressure, limiting the blood flow to the brain."

"What does that *mean*, Carter?" Every time he avoided her eyes, her insides felt like they were being ripped out. "Can you speak English?"

"I'm sorry, Bryce." He put his hands up to his face. His voice shook. "Your brain won't survive the lack of oxygen."

Bryce's angry heart stopped pumping. Her furious breaths were caught in her throat. The whole world was frozen.

"What are you saying?" she said, her words almost a gasp.

"You have less than a month to live."

Bryce closed her eyes. This wasn't happening. Maybe none of this was happening. Maybe this was another one of her visions. Maybe she was actually somewhere else. Her mind went to the morning of the CAT scan. She wished she had gone calmly into the machine and lain there peacefully as she listened to the radio. She would emerge from the scan without ceremony. Everything would be normal.

Bryce's eyes opened. Carter was still standing in front of her. It was real.

She had woken up a ghost of who she had been five years ago, and she was just starting to materialize now. She was just starting to live. How could she be dying?

He brought his hands down. His face was red, streaked with tears. "I think you should come in. To the hospital."

Immediately Bryce shook her head, backing away. She wouldn't go back there.

"Maybe there's something we can do. We can figure something out. We can study you. Bring in as many experts as it takes."

"Study me? Like one of your classes? No." If she was going to die, she wasn't going to do it between those walls. She would do it on her own terms.

"Medical observation, Bryce." He sounded aggravated, hurt.

"Get away from me," she said, and her breath came back. The beating heart came back, reminding her she was alive.

Bryce turned from Carter and walked away, her hand on her chest. She felt the wild thumping of her heart, the warmth of her skin beneath her dress.

"Bryce!"

He started to follow her, but she whirled around and shouted, "I need to be alone!"

His arm fell, his face fell.

Bryce turned to the stretching sidewalk and strode as quickly as her legs would allow. Soon, she no longer felt him behind her.

Good. She walked quicker. If all he was to her was a doctor, she didn't need him anymore. He couldn't save her. She thought about turning around, yelling that to his back, but what would be the point? She thought about yelling after him, telling him to come back. But he was gone.

Die, die, die. The word took a different meaning now. *I am going to die. Die* was a place just as much as a verb. A place she was going to, no matter which direction she went.

A wave of heat shot through her, pain coursing from her skull down her neck, her back, her spinal cord. The city turned on itself, the sidewalks rising before her.

Tall green grasses.

She was in her backyard. Her limbs came flopping out from under her, skinny and tanned. She was seven. Sydney came running up, her dark curls flying. "Got ya!" she shrieked, her fingers cocked in a gun. "Bang! Bang!" Instinctively Bryce's hand went to her bony chest, and she fainted to the ground.

She hit the ground, rolling around in the tall, sweet grass, letting the blades tickle her face.

"I'm dead," she said, and with a blink Bryce was back on the streets of downtown Nashville, her hand still on her chest. She lowered it, and her fingers touched cement. She was on her hands and knees again. Her head rebounded in pain with every heartbeat. She tried to take deep breaths, to calm herself, taking in the grainy sidewalk. A red spot landed on the rough gray. Another. She lifted her hand to her face. Blood was dripping from her nose.

Just need to walk it off. She stood up and wiped her nostrils with a Kleenex from her purse.

She looked up. The restaurant rose in front of her. She stuffed the tissue in her purse and opened the sleek glass doors to a warm room full of chattering people. They looked at her with smiles. A few said hello and waved at her to sit down next to them. She knew everybody, and everybody knew her.

But as Bryce stood there, shivering, she had never felt more alone.

CHAPTER TWENTY-SEVEN

Y ou've got to try this risotto, Bryce," someone was saying. Bryce was vaguely aware of a fork floating in front of her. She took it and set it on her plate.

"You've got to try it!" the voice said again. A perfumed head tilted in front of her. Zen.

Candlelight sparkled off of her loose curls. "Lost in space?" she said.

"Yeah," Bryce replied.

She popped the ricelike pasta in Bryce's mouth, an explosion of taste. It was delicious. Overwhelming.

The restaurant was painted in a warm red-orange color,

filled with candles and mirrors and dark wood. In the light, everyone—Zen, Mary, the brunettes, Greg's parents, Gabby's mother—looked like they were blushing. All the tables in the tiny restaurant, except for the booths by the wall, were combined in a long line where the wedding party sat.

Greg's parents, Jim and Lisa, were to the right of Gabby, next to their sons. Greg sat there, folding and refolding his cloth napkin into different shapes, seemingly oblivious to everyone around him.

Next to Greg was the broad-shouldered line of his fraternity brothers, including the tousle-haired Tom. He had given her a small wave when she walked in.

On the left side was Gabby's mother, then her grandparents, speaking mostly Spanish, and the bridesmaids. Gabby was radiant at the head of the table.

This morning at the rehearsal she wore her pearl-colored heels with a pair of jeans and a loose linen tank, hands shaking as she held a practice bouquet of prairie flowers that Mary picked from the church landscaping. Greg stood across from her, hair still bed-messed, and they muttered back and forth, quick, repeating, stumbling over the words like they were back in elementary school giving a book report.

Tomorrow the bridesmaids would meet early at the stone-carved church, to help Gabby get ready. The ceremony would start at 4 p.m., and after it was over, the hundred guests would go in caravan back to one of the lavish conference rooms at the Opryland Hotel. They had invited mostly family and friends from Nashville. Only a few other Stanford people were flying or driving in. The reception lasted from "6 p.m. till?" the invitation had said, like it could go on forever if they wanted it to.

As she thought of the invitation's question mark now, Bryce imagined it like the birth and death dates for famous figures from history or civics class. Abraham Lincoln (1809–1865). Martin Luther King, Jr. (1929–1968). Occasionally, you would look up someone who was still alive, and the dates were open-ended (1950–?).

Bryce's dates ended in a question mark, too. But not for long.

She wondered with a funny pang if Dr. Warren knew the approximate date of her death. Why stop at a wedding rehearsal? They could have a funeral rehearsal, too. She would test out the coffin, hear everyone say nice things, make sure they picked the right music. She laughed to herself at the thought, though it made her stomach turn.

Just the other day she was standing in the Saks dressing room with Gabby, trying on her bridesmaid dress and dreaming about her own wedding. And now . . . Bryce couldn't help it. More tears gathered in her eyes.

One of the brunettes leaned in, her manicured hand holding bread dipped in olive oil. "Save your tears for the toast, honey. A crying maid of honor always kills it."

No one had told her she had to make a toast. Maybe Gabby would let her off the hook because she knew how bad Bryce was at public speaking.

Elena, Gabby's mother, excused herself from a conversation with Greg's parents and approached their end of the table.

"Bryce, darling," she said, squatting down, her dark eyes shining. "How are you?"

"I'm good," Bryce said, composing herself.

The clinking of crystal sounded over the din. Gabby stood up, a glass of red wine in her hand. Elena smiled apologetically at Bryce and retook her seat.

As everyone brought their conversations to a close, Bryce glanced in front of her and realized her wineglass had been removed. That was thoughtful of them. But at this very moment, she wished they hadn't been quite so thoughtful.

"Mary, pour me a glass of wine, okay?" Bryce whispered as Gabby began speaking, telling the story of her and Greg's first date.

"But I thought—" she whispered back.

"One glass isn't going to kill me," Bryce said, pursing her lips.

"Are you sure?"

Zen, trying to listen to Gabby's speech, snatched the bottle, filled a generous glass, and placed it in front of Bryce. Mary shrugged and went back to listening.

"—and then, it was just like a movie. We had climbed down this cliff to an empty beach, and I didn't care that we were lost, or even that my pants were dirty."

The table tittered, the women among them wiped their eyes. Gabby had them in the palm of her hand. Bryce pushed out a real smile for her friend. Her lovely, entrancing friend.

"All I could see was Greg. And it's been the same ever since. To my darling husband-to-be, and to all of you!" Gabby finished, raising her glass. Bryce followed the rest of the table and raised her own, taking a sip. Her first glass of wine. It tasted like spicy, sour juice. She took another sip.

Suddenly, Zen was grabbing Bryce by the elbows, standing her up. "Maid of honor!" she cried.

"I don't have anything," she said in a low voice.

"Just say what you feel right now," Zen whispered.

Bryce floated above the faces in the dim light. Greg's groomsmen looked at Bryce, their polite smiles like carbon copies of one another, their toned arms crossed over their chests. Greg fiddled with his risotto. Bryce tightened her hand around the stem of the wineglass.

What she felt. "I can't tell you how happy I am to be here."

She stopped. That was supposed to sound like she was *actually* happy. She pushed on. "I remember the first time I heard Greg and Gabby were getting married. . . ." The sips of alcohol were swimming to her stomach like they had on that day at Los Pollitos. "We were at a restaurant and I had just, you know, come home. And I was happy for them."

Lies. Gabby's face twisted into a smile, trying to keep back tears.

"I'm happy for them now," Bryce continued.

Their lives stretched in front of them, and behind them. Bryce's life was another day gone.

"And I will always be happy for them. . . ." Her life was draining by the minute, by the second. And so was her blood. Isn't that what Carter said? Draining from her brain.

People were starting to fidget. Bryce swallowed her nerves. She should get it together. She didn't want to leave them with this impression of her. These sniveling, stumbling words. She took a deep breath.

"Gabby and Greg have been a blessing to me. They're my best friends. As you know, it's been an eventful few years for all of us." Scattered laughter. Bryce paused, looking into her glass. She looked up. "It's been amazing to have them around, to remind me of how great our pasts were. But I know the future's going to be even better. To Gabby and Greg," Bryce finished, because she didn't know what she was supposed to do at the end. She didn't know anything about any of this, and she needed some time. She needed more time.

Elena stood up and raised her glass with everyone at the table. Bryce set down her wine with a splash and made a beeline for the bathroom.

It was dark inside the small, tiled room. She couldn't find the light switch. She shuffled through the space, feeling tile after tile. Why couldn't she find one freaking light switch? She heard her own heavy breathing, scattered with sobs.

Someone turned on the light.

"Are you okay?" It was a man's voice. Greg.

"Yeah, I just need to wash my face," Bryce said tensely.

"I don't like it either, Bryce," he said, stepping farther inside, filling the room with the smell of cologne and his wine-stained breath. He looked toward the main room, and back to Bryce.

"Hear me out," he said. Bryce ran her hands under the

water, her vision blurred. She could feel his whispers on her neck. "I can't stop thinking about us. I think about my life with Gabby, and I think about what my life could be with you, and I always choose you. Always, and I always will."

Bryce turned off the water. Paper towels. Where were the paper towels? Greg turned her around and took her shoulders, breathing in her face. His eyes wouldn't leave hers, and she caught them, a blazing blue. He loosened his grip.

"Bryce, I don't believe you want this to happen any more than I do, so let's do something about it!"

"I'm not going to change my mind." Bryce shook him off and dried her hands on her dress. "And if you really didn't want to be here, you wouldn't be here."

He stood in the doorway, blocking her. "What do you mean?"

Bryce stood facing him, looking him straight in the eye. "I mean that if you really didn't want to be with Gabby, things would never have gotten this far. You wouldn't be at the rehearsal dinner the night before your wedding."

He said nothing. He backed down from the doorway. "I can't do it, Bry."

"I asked you this before, and I'll ask you again." Bryce

kept her voice low, under the din of the restaurant. "What do you want?"

"Honestly?" Greg grimaced. "I don't know." He hung his head.

Bryce didn't like to see him this way. She had cut herself off from him, but she had never stopped caring. He wasn't happy, she could see that.

She took his cheeks in her hands, not because she wanted him, but because she wanted him to do better.

"It's not just your life you're deciding here, it's Gabby's, too. And she deserves to be happy. She deserves her fairy-tale prince."

He just nodded, solemnly. There was wetness in the corners of his eyes.

She dropped her hands from his cheeks. There was nothing left in Bryce but heavy tiredness. She felt sucked dry. Emptied.

She walked past Greg's slumped figure, but before she hit the doors, she turned around. "You were going to be happy before me. Now be happy after me."

Outside she watched the traffic for a taxi. After several cars, she saw one speed through a yellow light a block away. With the hollow jolt of death in her, Bryce walked in front of the hurtling car.

Two feet in front of her, the cab screeched to a halt. "Are you crazy?" the driver yelled out his open window. "You wanna get killed?"

In answer, Bryce got inside and asked him to take her home.

CHAPTER TWENTY-EIGHT

The next day, Bryce woke up. What a miracle. Call the president.

During the ride home last night she had started laughing to herself about the ridiculousness of it all. The car pulled up to her house and she took out her money, laughing. She collapsed on her bed and laugh-cried herself to sleep. The driver must have thought she was out of her mind.

Well, she *was* out of her mind. Technically, since a little more than five years ago, she was.

Bryce had fallen asleep in her dress. She changed into

sweatpants, washed her face, grabbed her red gown in its Saks bag from her closet, and asked her mother for a ride.

Her mom greeted Bryce like it was any other morning, absently flipping through a design magazine. Dr. Warren must not have called them yet.

"Good luck, baby," she said when she pulled up to the church. "We'll be there for the ceremony."

"Bye, Mom," Bryce said, and kissed her on the cheek.

She refused to let her thoughts drift away from the wedding. Did she have her shoes? Yes. Did she remember how to walk down the aisle? One, together. Two, together. She approached the church's heavy wooden doors through the warm morning haze. They creaked open, and Bryce stepped into the velvety hush.

A silk white ribbon hung from the pews on either side of the church's center aisle—Gabby's path to the altar. She and Greg would stand between two huge, mounted bouquets of white roses. Beautiful. Bryce veered off to the right, to the side room where everyone would be getting ready.

At first she thought the beige room was empty; then she saw the bride sitting in the far corner. Her dress was thrown haphazardly across a chair, its full, creamy length on the carpeted floor like spilled milk.

"Hey!" Bryce called. "Where is everyone?"

Gabby didn't look up. Her hands stayed folded in her lap, hair falling around her face. Bryce walked over and kneeled beside her.

"What's wrong?"

"Don't," Gabby said quietly from behind the curtain of her hair.

"Don't what?"

She pulled back to face Bryce. She didn't look like herself. She looked like a wax version of Gabby, a permanent scowl on her tear-stained face. "The wedding's off."

"Oh!" Bryce let out a little cry. "Wha— why?"

"I don't know, Bryce," Gabby said quietly. "Why don't you tell me?" Her voice was tight, like coiled springs.

Bryce stood. An anvil dropped between them. An unmovable, unchangeable truth.

"I wish I had told you," Bryce said, backing up. Gabby followed Bryce with her eyes.

"How *could* you?"

"It was a huge, giant mistake." She was yanking the words out, pulling them like string, and none of what she was saying could ever be right.

"Which time?" Gabby's voice was like ice.

"What?"

"Which time was it a mistake?"

"Every time," Bryce said automatically.

"He still loves you."

"No, he doesn't. I told him to make you happy."

Gabby's eyes narrowed, her lip still trembling. "Too late."

Bryce wanted to disappear somewhere, blend into the air or the water.

Gabby got up, too, stepping away from the chair with her arms stiffly at her sides. Her feet scuffed the white patch of fabric on the ground.

"You're standing on your dress," Bryce said, feeling tears well up. She had ruined everything.

"Don't be an idiot." Gabby laughed bitterly.

The room was so silent then. So quiet. Bryce could hear cars pass by outside.

Gabby broke the silence, staring at the floor. "I guess since you haven't left yet, I could ask you why, but I think I kind of know why." She looked at Bryce with a small, sad smile, her eyes still narrowed. Bryce didn't understand.

Before she could muster up a reply, Gabby continued. "He was still yours, in your mind, wasn't he?"

"I don't know," Bryce said, shaking. She clenched her jaw, trying to control it.

"I feel sorry for you," Gabby said. She spoke slowly, drawing out each word.

"Don't," Bryce said. "It was my fault. I don't know what—" She stopped. She wished she could stop saying that. She didn't know *anything*. And it seemed like she never would.

"Listen," Bryce said, collecting herself.

"I don't have to listen to anything." Gabby jumped on Bryce's words.

"I'll be gone." The words rushed out of her. "I mean it. I'll leave you alone. You guys could work things out."

Gabby shook her head. "It's too late, Bryce." She gathered her dress in her arms and walked past Bryce to the door.

"Gabby, please," Bryce begged, but she didn't know what she was asking for. Gabby stopped in the doorway. "I'm sorry."

"Me too," she said.

Her footfalls echoed in the empty church, and the door swung open, creaking, and finally shut.

Soon Bryce left, too, leaving her gown on one of the pews as she exited through a side door. She didn't call her mom to pick her up.

The day was gray, her mind was gray.

None of it was hitting her, but not because she wasn't letting it. There was nothing left of her to absorb the impact. Bryce had done all the damage she could possibly do, and now everything was in pieces. Sometimes Bryce had to pause in the middle of a parking lot, or on someone's lawn, and wrap her arms around her stomach. She was falling apart, and the pieces were going to float away from her. Her arm would fall off first, then a leg, her head would drift up to the sky like a balloon.

The long, dry walk ended, and Bryce was home on River Drive, standing in front of the big blue house. Her fingers and toes were numb, and her limbs ached from tiredness. Her family was inside, laying out their clothes for a ceremony that wouldn't happen.

Bryce took a deep breath.

"Forgive me," she said out loud to everyone. To her family. To Carter. She walked up the sidewalk with the last ounce of energy she had left. All she wanted was to curl up under a blanket and hope that time passed quickly.

Forgive me.

CHAPTER TWENTY-NINE

Without going into too much detail, Bryce stepped into her house and announced the canceled wedding. She stood behind the couch, where her mother sat in a knee-length silk dress next to her father in his best suit.

"Why?" they had asked, worried.

"It'll blow over," Bryce had said listlessly. "I'm going outside."

Bryce had made it about halfway through the pasture before she collapsed on her knees. She lay in the grass, the grass where she and Sydney pretended to shoot each other with guns, and let tears run down her cheek into the dirt.

Bryce was dying. The sheer, hard fact of that would remain under everything she did, as if there was a voice that wasn't hers saying, "Remember?"

You're eating a bowl of cereal, Bryce. Cold milk and puffy, flavored corn. Will these half-digested Cocoa Puffs still be inside you when your stomach stops working? Will your heart be in midbeat, or will it have just finished one? Will you be thinking of Carter or your family? Or will you just be at the drugstore with your mom, expiring with a list of useless prescriptions in your hand?

The voice had infinite questions, but Bryce had no answers. The answers would only come with the thing itself.

Since she had found herself in a hospital bed, the thought of dying hadn't occurred to her once. It hadn't come to her in dark thoughts. It hadn't even come to her in visions. It had only been secondhand: In the tension behind everyone's words, in the fear running across their faces when she sat up or stood, in the way people she didn't know touched and talked to her, as if her closeness with death was the only thing about her they should pay attention to.

So she treated the thought of death like a piece of floating debris in her way at the lake. Like a crate of oranges knocked over in one of the aisles of the supermarket. It was a temporary obstacle she could overcome.

Bryce had learned to trust her body that way. If she did all the right things, it would take care of the rest. But she had remembered "the right things" too late. Somewhere, something had gone terribly wrong.

Bryce sat up in the pasture, her body feeling like a squeezed sponge, her skin as salty dry as the grass around her.

She headed back to the house.

Inside, her parents were still in their good clothes. Bryce heard electronic beats blaring faintly from Sydney's room.

"You both look so nice," Bryce said, emotion welling in her again. Her mother had put on pearls. Her father had once again forgotten to rinse a patch of shaving cream near his ear. "Why don't you guys go out for brunch?"

"What?" her mother scoffed, glancing sideways at her husband. "No."

"Yeah," Bryce said, putting on a big smile. "Take me to see Carter and go. It'll be fun. You probably haven't been out in forever. Go to the Opryland."

Bryce's mother swallowed, nodding. "We haven't. It's true, Mike."

"Let's do it," her father said quickly. His eyes were sparkling. "We might not look this presentable again for another year."

*

Thirty minutes later, Bryce watched her parents pull away from the Vanderbilt Medical Center parking lot. The overcast morning had changed into a sickly, clouded afternoon, where the sun burned the clouds' edges like toast, and even the birds were too choked with wet air to sing.

She passed through the sliding doors of the hospital, through the entryway lined by framed waterfalls, and ascended to the third floor with three quiet beeps of the elevator.

Carter wasn't here, Bryce knew that. He usually spent Saturdays at her house. Maybe he'd stop by the neurology wing in the evening to see Sam, but most likely he was at his apartment on campus, making himself an omelet. Doing his laundry. Staring at a book.

Dr. Warren had pulled up the shades in her office, bathing the room with gray light from the window. She was bent over her desk, immersed in paperwork. Bryce knocked on the door frame.

Dr. Warren looked up, her plucked eyebrows raised in surprise. "Bryce."

"We need to talk," Bryce said.

"All right." Dr. Warren got up from her desk, glancing around the dim office. "You know what? Let's eat."

✳

They sat on a bench facing a manmade pool, giant pretzels and hot cheese between them. Spanish moss climbed tree trunks behind their bench, twisting around the gnarled branches before it dropped green toward the shady trickle of the water.

After Bryce had chewed her last bite of pretzel, she turned to Dr. Warren. "So this is the part when you say 'I told you so,' right?"

Dr. Warren crossed one panty-hosed leg over the other. "I consider it my job to never have to tell anyone that." She sighed. "What did Carter tell you?"

"Everything."

Dr. Warren tossed the wax paper she was holding aside. Her steeled face was trying to hold back disappointment. "So you understand there's very little we could have done in the first place. The only 'I told you so' is perhaps that we could have known sooner."

Bryce looked guiltily out to the fountain. "And now I'm going to pay." A bitter laugh rose in her. "But not even me. My family . . ."

Tears stung Bryce's eyes for the third time that day, thinking of her parents waiting for her that morning. They had finally put on their good clothes again, and they were going out for a nice meal. Together. With a sob like a blow to her gut, Bryce imagined the day of her funeral. Her dad only owned one suit. He'd wear it that day, too.

Dr. Warren leaned toward her, putting a hand on her shoulder. "Don't think about that."

"I have to think about that," Bryce said, shaking her head. "I have to."

The doctor stayed silent, uncrossing her legs and leaning her forearms on her knees. She looked like an athlete, too, with her chopped hair and wiry frame. She squinted out at the park, trying to solve a problem that had already been solved.

"I haven't really thought of anyone but myself," Bryce said softly.

"I'd imagine it would be difficult not to," Dr. Warren responded. "You know, Bryce . . . it's funny, the way you resisted."

Bryce looked at the doctor, who was smiling to herself.

"No patient has ever been so feisty about her freedom. It made me look at all my patients differently. It made me remember that even though I know how to help them, I can't quite imagine what they're going through." Dr. Warren leaned back against the bench, her eyes still narrowed in focus, looking into Bryce's. "How would you like to move forward, Bryce?"

"You mean tell them?" Bryce felt her insides burn at the thought.

"There are counselors available. . . ."

"Dr. Warren?" Bryce interrupted. A flock of birds scattered from a nearby tree, matching Bryce's flurried thoughts. "I don't think I want to tell them at all."

The doctor looked at her sternly. "Are you sure?"

"I—" Bryce searched for the words, watching the birds reassemble around the pool, pecking at the water. "I don't want them to think they could do something when they can't. I don't want them to scramble around, trying to fix things, and argue about the right way to do it. I don't want them to spend any more time in the hospital. I want them to be happy. I'll have to lie to them, but at least they'll be happy."

She expected Dr. Warren to object, to insist that no, Bryce couldn't do this on her own. That the hospital should help them through this transition. All the things Bryce had heard before.

Instead, Dr. Warren's face broke into a sad smile. She lifted her arms and pulled Bryce to her chest. "All right, honey," she said. "All right."

Bryce allowed herself to stay next to Dr. Warren for a long time, and the doctor didn't let go either. They had always bumped heads, but the doctor had been steady for her in that way, like a rock she could never move. So Bryce just leaned against her now.

They got up to go and walked through the park's paths, Dr. Warren rolling up the sleeves of her linen blouse against the heat. Bryce decided she would call her parents and ride home with them. She wanted to hear about their date.

"If you need anything, you know where I am," the doctor said as she got into her car. "Things are going to get . . . harder in the next few weeks. I can help with that if you call me."

"Thank you, Dr. Warren."

"And take care, Bryce." She smiled. A breeze finally picked up, rustling the leaves above them.

I'll try, Bryce thought. I'll try.

CHAPTER THIRTY

Ready, aim, hit.

And hit. And hit. Bryce felt wood breaking little by little under the force of her blows, driving the nail deep. She'd been helping her dad fix up the barn, and the physical work felt good. Muscles in her shoulders that hadn't been used since five years ago, when she swam for three hours every day, were crying out in pain. But the ache was the equivalent of a stretch in the morning. It was a pure, happy ache of waking up. Sweat pricked her forehead.

The barn was shady and cooler than outside, but after an hour with the hammer Bryce was more heated and out

279

of breath than she should have been. She wasn't about to tell her dad that, though, hammering away next to her. She couldn't risk him asking why.

It had been a week since the canceled wedding, since she had spoken with Dr. Warren, and Bryce was starting to get headaches more often than she used to. Small, dull headaches that went away quickly. Her breath was getting short after she walked up the stairs.

There was no way she'd ruin everything by letting on, not after last week, when her dad surprised her mom with a trip to a bed-and-breakfast for their anniversary. They stole kisses in front of Sydney and Bryce, and when they waved from the car Sydney had graced her with one of her rare smiles.

She told Bryce last year at this time their mom completely forgot their anniversary. "Dad threw away the crappy bouquet he bought for her when she came into the kitchen to refill her wineglass. Neither of them said a word."

Sydney had stayed home a couple of nights last week. "I'm not going to leave an invalid all by herself," she had said, flopping on the couch in her thigh-high socks and enormous T-shirt, this one covered in a picture of Courtney Love collapsed onstage.

"I'm not an invalid," Bryce had protested. She wondered if Sydney had noticed she was starting to move slower these days, to match her lungs. But Syd just smiled and tossed her the remote.

✳

The barn was really starting to shape up. Bryce pounded in the last nail on a long row and stepped back to admire the job. In one Saturday she and her dad had managed to replace most of the rotting beams in the walls and floors. It looked a bit patchy with the bright yellow of the new wood standing out from the rest, but it didn't smell like mold anymore.

"Now, what about the plane?" Bryce sidled up to her dad, nudging him with her elbow.

He put his arm around her. "We'll see, Brycey. We'll see."

She helped him pack up his tools, and they headed into the house. They'd been at it all day, and it was getting dark.

When they got in, Sydney was padding around the halls in various stages of dress, digging through drawers for eyeliner or jewelry. She scurried around while Bryce ate dinner with her parents, shoving the contents of her plate into her mouth before applying lipstick.

Bryce flopped on the couch with a bowl of M&M's and *The Adventures of Huckleberry Finn*. She was *really* reading it this time, not just for school. She was putting herself into the story, the way Sam would imagine it. If she could picture his peaceful face, the story unfolding under his closed eyes, it made her feel better about whatever was waiting for her.

"Bryce." Bryce followed the path of Sydney's fishnetted legs up to her made-up face. "Can I borrow your pearl earrings?"

"What for?" Bryce asked. But she knew what for.

"I was thinking about putting them in my soup," Sydney said sarcastically.

Bryce filtered a handful of M&M's in her mouth, excluding the red ones, which she hated. "No, Syd. I'm sorry. You may not wear my vintage pearl earrings."

"Ugh!" Sydney protested. "Why not?"

Bryce stood up. "Because I'm going to wear them."

"To read *Huck Finn*?"

"No, silly!" Bryce pinched her sister's cheeks. "I'm going out with you!" She brushed past Sydney toward the kitchen.

"Bry— this . . ." Sydney started. "This is a bad idea."

"It's a fantastic idea! I wanna see your world, Syd." Bryce made an arc over her head with her hand, face frozen in a dramatic, Judy Garland smile. She was imitating Sydney back when she was a little girl, back when she wanted to be a Broadway star. "I want to see the world over the rainbow!"

Sydney snorted, shaking her head. "You're a freaking nut job."

"I approve." Bryce heard her mom's voice from behind the couch. "You two could use some time out of the house together."

Sydney turned around in shock. Bryce looked back at her mom. "Really?"

Their mother nodded, humming the first few notes of "The Hustle." She'd had a glass of wine with dinner.

Bryce looked at Sydney, her eyebrows raised. "How often is *that* going to happen? Now I have to come out."

Sydney surrendered. "You have five minutes."

Bryce took the stairs slowly. She couldn't help imagining with a pang what she would be doing tonight if she and Carter were still talking. Maybe ride out to the Big Chief Drive-In. The outdoor movie theater was one of the last ones left in Tennessee, with all of its old neon and rusty decorations from the fifties. When the nights were hot and the mosquitoes weren't too bad, they sat on top of his car, drinking slushies. The whole night when they kissed he tasted like blue-raspberry.

"Stop," she whispered aloud, throwing on her blue dress from the rehearsal dinner and her bridesmaid heels. *Stop thinking about Carter.* He knew what was happening to her, and they couldn't hide from it. Seeing each other would only cause them both more pain.

"And what time will you be home?" their mother was saying when Bryce came upstairs.

"One a.m.," Sydney said. "Now please move, we're going
to be late!" They could hear the engine of her friend's blue
muscle car humming outside.

Bryce's mom stepped aside and swept to kiss her youngest daughter's cheek as she went through the door. Then she
kissed Bryce.

"Be careful," she said.

By the time they scrambled down the sidewalk and
shoved themselves into the backseat, Bryce's breaths were
coming thin and painful. She closed her mouth, trying to
bring in air through her nose. This was definitely a bad idea.
But something made her come out.

Maybe it was the way her parents' footsteps drifted from
above down to her room, the sounds of them being and talking. Or the fact that she hadn't bothered to fill her drawers
with any pants or long-sleeved shirts for fall, because she
didn't know if she was going to wear them.

She would make this worth it.

In the car, Sydney didn't acknowledge Bryce. Either she
was mortified by her dorky older sister or she just couldn't
hear her over the roaring engine and chest-rattling bass beat.

Bryce rolled down the window a crack to get some fresh

air. Sydney's friends were all boys, skinny with tattoos and hairstyles slicked back like James Dean.

They pulled up to a red brick warehouse in a row of identical-looking warehouses. They were in Nashville's industrial district, or what was left of it. The only thing to distinguish their spot from the rest of the sprawling buildings was a huge, red number *2* painted above a slatted metal door.

Bryce got out and Sydney motioned to her friends to go inside. Bryce was about to tell her not to worry, she'd be in the back, when Sydney said, "This is Lounge Two. This is where I work." Sydney put a cigarette between her lips and lit up.

"Work?" Bryce's eyes widened. Sydney let out a loud, barking laugh.

"Chill, Bryce. This isn't a strip club, it's a music venue." She spoke in a voice Bryce didn't fully recognize but didn't dislike, either. It was tough. Professional.

Bryce's face grew hot. "I didn't think it was a strip club!"

"I go around the club and get people's drink orders when there's a show."

"Is there a show tonight?"

"Every weekend. A DJ set. And you're lucky, this one's amazing. He's from South London."

"Why haven't you told Mom and Dad?"

At the mention of their parents, Sydney tensed, taking a

deep drag. "They stopped giving a shit about anything after your accident, Bryce. And this place was my saving grace. Swear to God. I mean, yeah, drinking is kind of part of the job. Customers want to take shots with you, you do it. But they're going to make me a bartender when school starts, and they've already booked a few bands I found online. They like me here, Bryce." Sydney's face lit up. "They think I have good taste in music."

"That's . . . that's awesome, Syd," Bryce said, meaning it. She felt proud. "But you should tell Mom and Dad. Especially now that"—she swallowed back dark thoughts—"now that things seem to be getting better."

"Yeah." Sydney stamped out her cigarette under her heel. "Hmm."

"They won't freak out about it, you're going to be eighteen."

"Shh . . ." Syd looked around. "Twenty-one. I'm twenty-one."

Bryce couldn't help but laugh as they headed toward the door. "So you've been twenty-one for three years now?"

Sydney laughed with Bryce, putting her arm around her waist. "Eternal youth, sis. Eternal youth."

The door opened and they were lost in sound pumping from endless speakers, sound she couldn't help comparing to a thousand cicada melodies, amplified, buzzing, dipping in and out and dripping down like drops of drum rain. She could actually see the tones around her, floating in the air and humming around her, looking like the translucent, shimmering bubbles she used to blow as a little girl.

A tall, skinny, tattooed guy bobbed over a laptop, brushing his hand on a turntable in a jerky rhythm. The dance floor was full of everyone from Vanderbilt sorority girls in peachy dresses to guys in Atlanta Hawks jerseys with cornrows.

Bryce slipped onto a bar stool near where Sydney was clocking in and took the frosty martini glass she slid toward her.

"Lemon drop," she said as she loaded a tray with drinks.

It was exactly that, in liquid form. Sweet, tart, bouncing on Bryce's tongue. She nodded her head to the beat and realized in the last half hour, she hadn't thought once about empty drawers.

An hour later, after her third lemon drop, Bryce was on the dance floor, smashing against sweaty bodies. She was gasping for breath, but so was everyone else. The beats had sped up, still steady, still rolling and swooping like a roller coaster. Everyone jumped with them. The lights flashed so fast it was as if Bryce were dancing slow.

Sydney appeared, the bright strobe catching her in choppy poses as she approached. The beat got faster. Bryce bobbed and weaved with the best of them.

"Bryce!" Sydney yelled.

"Syd!" Bryce yelled back. "I'm having so much fun!" Her lungs seized up, squeezing, so she stopped jumping. It was nothing worse than a 100-meter freestyle, she told herself.

"Awesome!" Syd replied. "Hey, so, I'm starving and I have a quick break. We're going to get something to eat. You wanna come?"

"No, thanks!" Bryce yelled. "I think I'm gonna have another drink!"

"Okay." Syd squeezed Bryce's arm. "Take it easy, okay? I'll be back in five."

She disappeared in the bumping bodies.

Bryce looked for the direction of the bar, finally spotting it. She took a step. The floor tilted. "Uh-oh," she muttered.

That old, familiar feverish feeling crept up her body, and she couldn't tell the difference between the strobe light and the flickering of her eyesight. Each beam burst with pain like needles in her eyes. The lights wouldn't stop. They were cutting red in her eyes. She tried to signal the person next to her, but she couldn't quite find her arms in the numbing heat that was spreading from her spine.

Bryce tried to take another step, but she was no longer in Lounge 2.

A loud car, the engine thundering.

It was the same car they were in tonight, and they were speeding along the streets of Nashville. The bass was bumping. The wheels swerved between the yellow lines, barely screeching to a stop at a red light. The driver, one of the tattooed James Deans, turned to the passengers, asking for directions to McDonald's. He tripped over his words, giggling, and the whole car stank of a bottle of vodka spilled on the floor of the backseat.

The laughing faces looked familiar. Bryce drew in breath in horror; she had seen this vision before. The dark-haired person next to her—

Sydney.

Sydney laughed at her friend driving, telling him to watch the road. At least that was what Bryce thought she was saying. Every second, the bass rattled her chest, and there were no other sounds. Sydney was laughing. The laughter like broken glass. Glass, shattering. And there, just as it had come to her in the CAT scan, was a sharp, sinking feeling that everything here was wrong.

Sydney had to get out of the car. *She had to.*

Bryce tried to pull her away, to open the door, to yell, but she was only half there. Another nauseous wave and Bryce pounded on the invisible barrier between Sydney and herself.

"Get out! Stop the car!" Bryce screamed.

But she didn't hear her. No one did.

The car lurched into motion and the vision snapped away. Bryce was lying on the sticky floor of Lounge 2, a circle of figures bent over her, shaking her shoulders, calling things she couldn't make out.

"I'm all right," she said. "I'm all right."

She stood up, and the crowd of people dispersed, dissolving into the music. Her head felt heavy with heat and pain, and the sight of the swerving car came to her in a flash of hot pain. Was it real? How much time had passed? Was it already happening?

Where was her sister?

"Do you know Sydney?" Bryce turned to the first person near her, a short girl with bleached-blond hair.

"No, honey, but are you okay? Your nose is bleedin'. . . ."

Bryce put her tongue up to lick away the blood. It tasted like sticky, salty metal. She wiped the rest away. There was a lot of it.

"Where's my sister?" Bryce yelled over the girl, turning to anyone else who would listen. "Does anyone know if Sydney left?"

Bryce pushed through the bodies to the door, her feet

returning in pinpricks of feeling. The bearded, large bouncer sat on a stool, counting money. "Did you see if Sydney left?"

He didn't look up. He pointed outside.

She pushed open the heavy metal slats and looked wildly around. The air felt like it had gotten frigid, and for some reason smelled like snow. Bryce licked away more blood. A door slammed down the street. It was the B60.

"SYDNEY!" Bryce screamed. Her sister's name echoed down the row of empty buildings. Bryce started hobbling toward the car in her heels. She didn't care how she looked. "Sydney, stop!"

Sydney stood up from the backseat, her arm draped over the door. "Bryce, Jesus. What?"

Bryce leaned on the car, wheezing. "Don't get in."

Her eyes darted to the driver. Sydney glanced, too. He looked calm, sober. When Sydney looked away, though, he brought a hand up to his mouth, burping. He was clearly amused with himself.

"Did you run into something? Go inside and wash your face."

"No!" Bryce shook her head. "I won't. You come with me." She sounded like a stubborn kid, but she couldn't get out much more. Her thoughts were trudging through the alcohol.

Sydney rolled her eyes. "Bryce, I'll be five minutes. We're just going to get some fries."

But Bryce couldn't forget the feeling, the incredible urge to get Sydney out, out, out. Pounding on the glass. The terrible lurch forward. Glass, and red. How could she explain?

Sydney sat in the backseat, pulling the door gently away from Bryce. She wasn't coming. Bryce would stand in front of the car if she had to.

"You have to take me home!" Bryce blurted out. "I'm sick. I've got a bloody nose. Please. I'm not feeling well."

Sydney sighed. "You can't wait five minutes?"

"No, now." Bryce grabbed her arm and yanked her from her seat. Sydney's foot kicked an open bottle and vodka sloshed out all over the floor. Bryce gripped Sydney tighter.

Bryce was panting, her makeup running in sweat down her face. Sydney shrugged at the driver.

"I guess I'll see you later, Jack."

The engine revved and the little blue car streaked down the street, the other backseat passenger slamming the door as it sped away.

Bryce's muscles relaxed. She let go of Sydney's hand. Warmth was creeping back into her limbs.

"Now what?" Sydney turned to Bryce. "You want to go

home? I don't suppose you've acquired a car in the hour we were here."

Bryce clutched for her purse, but it wasn't there. She looked at Sydney, whose phone was tucked in her leggings.

Bryce called 411 on Sydney's phone as her sister looked at her and smoked a cigarette, puzzling.

"City and state?"

"Nashville, Tennessee."

I do my best studying in the middle of the night, he told her once when they were entwined in the grass. *When nothing is awake but my brain.*

"What listing?"

"Vanderbilt Medical Center."

After speaking with the front desk and the confused night nurse at the neurology wing, Bryce got connected to Sam's room. The line rang and rang. Her heart sank. He wasn't there. But then, a click.

"Hello?" Carter whispered.

Bryce felt a smile growing wide on her face. "I had a feeling you were there."

Sydney cleared her throat, making a "get on with it" motion with her hands.

"Can you pick us up?" She told him where they were, and that it was an emergency. She hung up and they waited.

But it wasn't an emergency anymore. Sydney was there, next to her. That's what she was telling herself, trying to slow her frantic heart as the heat crept up her spine again, dotting her vision in black. She tried to breathe normally.

"Bryce?"

She held on to Sydney's arm, trying to keep her balance. She lost her sight, her feeling, no longer sure if she was vertical. In a blur, the pavement swerved toward her.

CHAPTER THIRTY-ONE

Don't ever do that to me again."

Sydney, Carter, and Bryce sat at the Grahams' kitchen table. They'd had a quiet car ride home.

"I thought you were about to go into another coma." Sydney was drinking tea, her pale hands wrapped tightly around her mug. She kept sneaking glances at Bryce when she thought her sister wasn't looking.

"I'm sorry," Bryce said. She couldn't say it enough. She shouldn't have gone out, she shouldn't have drank, she shouldn't have gotten herself worked up enough to pass out on the sidewalk.

As soon as Bryce had hit pavement, she was awake. The first words out of her mouth were, "Don't take me to the hospital."

Maybe it was the way Bryce had clutched her, or that Carter had pulled up seconds later, but Sydney had listened. Now she finished her tea and went to bed without a word.

Carter looked at Bryce, his eyes searching. He scooted his chair close to Bryce's, and laid his hands on its surface, waiting.

"I'm sorry to you, too," Bryce said.

"For what?" Carter said simply, his palms turned up briefly.

Bryce put her hand in his.

For the first time in what seemed like forever, she saw his smile. His blue-gray eyes were bright. With his other hand he reached toward his pocket, where he kept his Vanderbilt Medical ID card clipped to the fabric.

He unclipped it and threw it across the room.

*

In the morning, Bryce's floating mood was punctured by the sight of Sydney in her same spot at the kitchen table, head slumped in her arms. Her shoulders shook with sobs.

Under her folded arms was the local paper.

THREE KILLED IN DRUNK DRIVING ACCIDENT, the headline screamed. Underneath it, among the three school photos, was Sydney's friend Jack. Bryce drew in a breath.

Her vision had been real. She was right to keep Sydney out of that car. She swallowed, relief mingled with sadness washing over her.

Bryce put a hand on her sister's shoulder. Sydney grabbed it and squeezed. Bryce didn't need much else. She had kept her alive, and that was enough.

She helped Sydney back to bed, and then Carter came over. Though it was sprinkling lightly, they sat outside, the mist coating their warm skin. Bryce wrapped her arms around him and buried her face in his shirt.

"So tell me," he whispered.

"Tell you what?"

"Tell me how you knew to keep Sydney out of that car."

The wind swept through, and droplets of water landed in her eyes. She huddled further into him, not answering.

"Or you could tell me how you knew I sat with you while you were sleeping," he said, his fingers under her chin, bringing her out of the folds of his arms. "Or why the CAT scan broke."

Bryce sighed. *Don't tell Dr. Warren* sounded too much like *Don't tell Mom.* She sat up as he narrowed his eyes at her.

"My family doesn't need any more trouble," she said.

"I know," he said.

"Good." They were clear.

Bryce started at the beginning, from the moment she

woke up. The sharp filter on the world, the strange sights, the feeling that things weren't quite right. She told him everything. Every little detail, from the heated pain to the visions moving her forward and backward in time, putting her in places she'd never been before. When she finished, she felt like seven layers of heavy skin were peeled off her body. She was bare, yes, but she was free.

"So tell me," Bryce echoed, willing with every ounce of her that he wouldn't pick her up right then and carry her back to the hospital for another CAT scan. "What does it mean?"

But Carter was lost in thought. "So that's why your brain activity spiked so rapidly."

He grasped the sides of Bryce's head suddenly, looking back and forth between her eyes. His intensity made her laugh. But she was curious.

"Is there an answer?"

"No," he said, letting go, brushing her hair from her face. "Neuroscience has always said the human brain is hard-wired, permanent by the time we're adults. But there are also studies that say the brain has the ability to change structure and function in response to experience. When the brain suffers trauma it has the ability to rezone itself."

Carter paused, taking in her confused expression. "It's like after your accident, your brain was a puzzle, adjusting the shape of its pieces and how they fit together, but creating the same overall picture."

"Oh," Bryce said.

He was getting excited. "Experiences could be registered more or less intensely, with different emotional and even sensory reactions. Memories could be stored differently, released differently. Understanding changes, perception changes. Your perception could have been replaced by what you imagined others to see."

He stood up, pacing around the blue rectangle of the pool.

"Everyone's brain is trained to think linearly in time, but yours could have been rewired to understand time in a webbed or networked fashion, moments becoming linked less by cause and effect, and more by objects, words, other emotional triggers."

Bryce sat on the pool chair, her apparently miraculous head resting in her hands. Dried leaves skittered across the tarp. Carter had paced all the way to the other end, standing near the unused diving board.

"But what's the point of all this if I'm going to die?" Bryce called.

His face looked pained, but his body remained stiff, upright. He slowly made his way back to her, sitting in a neighboring pool chair, his legs stretched in front of him.

"Maybe you won't die," he said lightly.

"You said my brain wouldn't survive the swelling," she said.

He looked away.

Bryce had had plenty of time to come to terms with this fact. She had hit out her doom with a hammer, cut it away with a saw, walked with it past the Grahams' property until her legs were too weak to stand. Carter had not.

He looked back at her, squinting. "You remember things from when you were asleep?"

Bryce nodded.

"Tell me about one of the articles I read to you. The one about insects."

"I can't just pull things out of my head," she said.

"Try. It was in one of those nature magazines for kids. It was all there was around to read that day because I read you everything else."

Bryce closed her eyes. She thought about her hospital room, the blue curtain, the white ceiling, the circular lights. With a quick streak of pain, Carter was next to her, his face fuller than it was now, younger, wearing a T-shirt and shorts because the room was sweltering on a sticky summer day.

"Uhh . . ." he was saying, flipping through a faded magazine. "Let's see."

He settled on a page. "Want to learn about cicadas?" he asked Bryce.

She watched his face as he read, fascinated with this

version of Carter just barely out of his teenage years, deciding to spend a summer day at the bedside of a girl he didn't know, might never know.

"Cicadas are one of the longest-living insects. You may know them from the buzzing sound coming from certain trees as they emerge each summer. That sound is their legs rubbing together, communicating with each other after they have spent the winter underground."

Each word coming out of Carter's mouth was one Bryce knew better than the last. She began to speak along with him as he read.

"'Some cicadas can live up to seventeen years underground, slowly growing from babies to adults. They read the temperature of the ground in cycles to know when the years have passed. When it's time, they emerge from their holes to mate as beautiful, fully winged adults. . . .'"

Bryce was in the backyard again now, the heat of her head morphing with the fading heat of the September afternoon, quoting the article to Carter, tears pricking her eyes.

"'Once their purpose is fulfilled, they die, leaving the earth as quickly as they came.'"

Carter looked tired, brushing her cheek with his hand. Then he wrapped his arms around her like he would never let go.

CHAPTER THIRTY-TWO

Bryce was painting by numbers with her mother. Well, her mother wasn't painting by numbers; she was painting freehand from a photo of a Swedish winter landscape she found in *National Geographic*. She swirled blue and white to make an icy gray, and used tinges of purple for the shadows. That's why her mother was so good with color, Bryce knew. She remembered her trying to get Sydney and Bryce to paint pictures when they were kids. But Sydney was more interested in perfecting her version of "America, the Beautiful," and all Bryce wanted to do was run around catching bugs.

Bryce had spotted an art supplies store in a little nook near the Vanderbilt campus, and asked Carter to stop the car for a second. She had no idea where to begin buying paints, so she chose the most colorful box. And then, thinking about how angry she got when she wasn't good at things like art, Bryce threw in a couple of paint-by-numbers kits to boot.

Her mother had gotten home from an appointment to find tempera paints, paper, and Bryce at the dining room table, filling in a picture of a basket of kittens.

"Want to join me?" Bryce had asked.

Her mother had burst into nervous laughter. "I haven't painted in . . . God knows . . ." But she picked up a paintbrush lovingly.

"At least you're good at keeping inside the lines," her mother joked later, leaning over from her Swedish mountains.

"Yeah, if you want a lesson from me in kittens, just ask," Bryce said with a smirk.

Her mom chuckled.

Bryce glanced at the *National Geographic* photo again. Pure white snow coated a tall, imposing mountain range. The Alps. Gabby and Greg had seen them in person.

Gabby.

With a last flourish on one of the kitten tails, Bryce

whipped out her phone. She would see her friend one more time, she hoped. Bryce dug her teeth into her lip and typed, *Coffee?*

It took a little while, but finally, the answer was yes.

✱

Bryce was glad the café had a wall full of windows. It was a shame not to be outdoors on such a beautiful autumn day. Having only a thin pane between her and the orange leaves and cool breeze was the next best thing. Bryce had arrived early to get some iced tea and a scone, and to read. Thanks to Carter's extended study hours, she was now halfway through *The Adventures of Huckleberry Finn*. But she was having a hard time keeping her heart with Huck and the circus this morning.

People rushed in and out of the café, grabbing coffee and loading themselves into cars strapped with canoes and inner tubes. It was a beautiful Saturday, and everyone was scrambling to soak up the air they'd missed, holed up in their cubicles.

The door chimed. Bryce sat up in her chair. Gabby stepped inside. She had cut her hair, and her brown eyes looked brighter now, her cheekbones sharper, without a dark curtain or a winding braid. She looked around.

"Over here," Bryce called from the window. She shoved

away the little shivers of nervousness she felt when she saw her friend. There wasn't enough time left to be scared or worried. Gabby would forgive her, or she wouldn't, but either way, Bryce would tell her how she felt. She could at least do that.

When Gabby spotted Bryce, her lips turned up in a smile. She wore a cardigan over her long linen tank, and jeans paired with ballet flats. When she slipped into the seat across from Bryce, she looked happy. Her face was full. Her cheeks had color.

Gabby set her hands in front of her, folded. She looked at Bryce, waiting.

"You look great," Bryce said, putting her own hands around her glass of iced tea, glancing at the crescent lemon that drifted around the edges. "I like your hair."

"Thank you," Gabby said.

Bryce took a breath. "I called you here because I wanted you to know that I'm so sorry. The sorriest I've ever been in my whole life," Bryce added slowly. "I also wanted to say you were right about me being confused. I know it's no excuse, but . . . I was so confused. I was mixed up about the past and the present." Bryce stopped, staring into Gabby's eyes, which seemed to be looking through her. She swallowed. "I should have just told you how I felt. About the whole thing. About how hard it was to see you two together. I know it was still so wrong. I'm sorry. I can't say it enough."

Gabby gave her a sad smile. "What's done is done."

Bryce began to respond, but Gabby held up a hand. Bryce stayed silent.

"I wasn't marrying Greg to hurt you, but I did. I see that now. And I'm sorry about that, too."

Bryce shook her head. "We both ended up getting hurt, I think."

Gabby responded with a nod, her hands still folded. Neither of them said a word for a long time. Cars came and went. The door opened and shut. Bryce wondered if that was all. She wondered if Gabby would leave now. This could be the last time she ever saw Gabby. The girl whose laughter filled up even the largest room. The thought of ending things like this made Bryce squirm with pain.

"Can we . . ." Bryce finally spoke up. "Start over?"

Gabby's head tilted. She thought for a moment, her eyes bright. Her hands flattened on the table. "I think so," she said with a smile.

Bryce raised her eyebrows, breaking into disbelieving laughter. "Really?"

Gabby shrugged. "You know I can't hold grudges." She broke off a piece of Bryce's scone and popped it into her mouth. "Besides, something tells me it wouldn't have worked out anyway with Greg," she said with a bitter smile. "Guess where our dear friend is now?"

"I don't know," Bryce said, leaning forward. He hadn't contacted her.

"Me neither," Gabby said, nodding at the look of surprise on Bryce's face. "Right?"

"He didn't tell you?"

"He took his grandmother's old van and all his camping stuff. He won't answer anyone's calls."

Bryce rolled her eyes. He had dreamed of new inventions and trips to space and questions like whether colors could match up with sounds. Maybe he was better off sailing from one new landscape to another.

Gabby laughed and Bryce joined in. As her shoulders heaved, she fought to conceal the pain shooting through her chest. These days, Bryce got a little dose of pain every time she did anything besides sitting. She shrugged it off. Her heart was soaring.

"He wasn't ready for either of us," Gabby said thoughtfully, their laughter fading.

Bryce lifted her iced tea in agreement, then told Gabby about Carter and the "senior prom," and her night out with Sydney, minus the vision and the blood.

Gabby said they could go out whenever she came back to visit, but she was leaving tomorrow for D.C.

"You're going, then?" Bryce had allowed herself to hope that now that Gabby was back, she'd be there with her until the very end.

"I sure am," Gabby answered. "I won't be able to start until second semester, but this way I can get my bearings before I start school."

"You're going to live there all by yourself?"

Gabby looked at Bryce as if she should know the answer. "You told me I could do it! Don't go back on me now."

"Of course not," Bryce pushed out. "I just wondered if things might have changed. . . ."

"Well." Gabby paused, smiling to herself. "I don't want to bring up the past again, but . . . sometimes when something bad happens in a place, you want to get away from it as soon as it happens. You know?"

"Yeah," Bryce said, swallowing tears. No tears. Not today.

She hadn't gotten to know the grown-up Gabby for long, but Bryce knew she'd do well up there. She had a way of winning people over, of making them feel good about themselves without even trying. She was smart enough that she'd move up in her class. She'd ace her exams, and then she'd meet someone at a function, and they'd give her a job on the spot because of the way she carried herself, like she already knew she'd been chosen for it.

She was the girl who could rock a tiara at a club and consume a three-hundred-page novel in a day. She was the girl who could lift herself out of the muck and forgive a betrayal from her closest friend, just like that.

Bryce wrapped her arms around Gabby and held her tight until she moved to go.

She held Bryce's hands for a squeeze, and turned to the door. "See you soon, Bry! I'll call you from D.C."

The door chimed closed.

Bryce watched Gabby through the wall made of windows for the last time. Through the leaf-filled parking lot, into her black VW, seat belt on, checking her mirrors.

Maybe Bryce would see her again. Not in Nashville, Tennessee, but maybe.

Gabby reversed and pulled away.

Maybe somewhere else, Bryce thought.

CHAPTER THIRTY-THREE

Bryce looked in the mirror. Her hair had grown to the middle of her back. It's my twenty-third birthday. Weird. She tried it aloud.

"It's my twenty-third birthday."

Bryce had pledged not to think about her death a month ago, but she couldn't help it. She thought about it today.

Well, there actually wasn't much to think about. It hadn't come, that was the main point. Four weeks had passed since the night Carter told her; then five weeks had passed. Now the month of September was long gone.

Bryce was still getting headaches and becoming short of

breath, but she had trained herself to take everything slow. Nobody expected her to be fast anymore, anyway, so it was easy to lie low. She remembered to bring everything she needed from downstairs up the stairs in one trip. She took a lot of hot baths. Sydney had stopped going out every night once school started, so Bryce didn't need to make any excuses for why she was staying in.

If not for the occasional look from Carter, she might have even forgotten that time was running out. With all the rest Bryce was getting, she had very little stress. Without stress, she had no visions.

She didn't miss the burning pain, but she had to admit she missed the memories. She didn't care about seeing the future, or whatever it was she saw. Five minutes from now, Bryce would be eating Carter's birthday breakfast of chocolate chip pancakes and applewood-smoked bacon. That was her future.

"There's the birthday girl!" Bryce's mom greeted her.

Her dad was leaning over the counter, reading the paper. "Do you have comfortable clothes on?" Aside from a bear hug, that was his only birthday greeting.

"When do I not?" Bryce asked, confused. "Why do you ask?"

"You'll see," he said, rubbing his hands together.

"No no no . . ." Bryce heard from the stove. Carter was overseeing Sydney as she worked the bacon. "Don't flip it. It doesn't have the right crispiness. You can tell by the bubbles."

"Just stick to your pancakes and let me do my job," her sister muttered. "Oh, hey, Bryce."

"Bryce!" Carter lit up, crossing the kitchen with batter stains on his shirt. He still refused to wear an apron, greeting her with a savoring hug and a kiss that said he hadn't seen her in years. The same way he did every day.

"Sit, sit, sit." Bryce's mother ushered her to the table.

No one was allowing Bryce to do any work in the kitchen. But that meant they weren't allowing her to sneak handfuls of chocolate chips, either.

Bryce looked over her shoulder to Sydney, who was avoiding crackles of bacon grease with her tongs in the air.

"Did you get the present I left on your bed?" Bryce called.

"You're not supposed to get other people presents on your own birthday," Sydney said, flipping a strip of bacon. "Only old people do that."

Bryce took this to mean yes. While Carter studied at the Vanderbilt Library yesterday, Bryce had finished with Huck Finn and wandered over to the computers, searching until she found what she was looking for. Last night before Sydney got home, Bryce left a printout on her pillow.

SAVANNAH COLLEGE OF ART AND DESIGN—PRODUCTION. SOUND DESIGN. PERFORMING ARTS. MUSIC MANAGEMENT.

Sydney gave her sister a one-sided smile over the stove. She'd consider it on her own time, but Bryce at least wanted her to know that when she got tired of the Nashville industrial district, there were options. It wasn't much, but it was something. Moving her in the right direction. She knew what it was like to get caught up in your own little world.

Bryce's thoughts were interrupted by scuffles and whispers. She started to turn around.

"Don't!" a chorus of voices let out.

Bryce snickered and obediently stayed put.

She had given her parents a present, too, but she knew they wouldn't accept it on what was supposed to be "her" day, so she just set it on the mantel. She wondered when they would notice the framed original of their prom picture, back out of storage, next to a framed print of the picture Bryce took of them. They had gotten the pose exactly identical. In love, then and now.

Two flicks of a lighter. A whispered, "One, two, three . . ."

"Happy birthday to you . . ." Her father's deep, out-of-tune voice stuck out from the chorus of Sydney, her mom, and Carter singing to her.

Bryce turned around. Her mother held a tall stack of

chocolate chip pancakes with two candles stuck in them. Bryce laughed and put her hands on her mouth. "Oh, yum!"

She could almost taste the melted chocolate. Everyone stood around her.

Bryce closed her eyes to make a wish, but she was coming up blank. She couldn't think of anything. She squeezed her eyes tighter and gave a nervous smile, knowing they were waiting on her. But everything seemed to have fallen from the sky exactly how it should have, even the bad stuff. This is how it was, and she couldn't imagine it any better.

Carter touched her shoulder. Bryce opened her eyes to the two bright flames. She enjoyed the sight of them flickering, bright and alive, and then she blew them out.

Soon the clatter of forks and knives joined the chatter of stuffed mouths, and everyone had to tell Carter to shut up when he started criticizing his own cooking.

"So," Carter finally changed the subject, biting off a strip of bacon. "Jane's expecting a visit sometime. They have a card for you in the neurology wing."

"You told them it was my birthday?" Bryce looked at him accusingly.

He winked at her. "They have your paperwork, Bryce. They know your DOB."

"Well played," Sydney said, popping a bite of pancake into her mouth.

"Yeah." Carter cleared his throat. "My dad and I . . . were there, and spoke to them yesterday."

Bryce put down her fork. "Your dad?"

"Yes, where is this mysterious father and when do I get to ask him which sports teams he supports?" Bryce's father asked between chews.

Bryce's gaze was locked on Carter across the table. He hadn't mentioned his dad visiting Sam. Was he happy about it? She couldn't tell.

"Well," Carter said, returning Bryce's look with a small smile, "you may run into him over there if you're back at the hospital sometime."

"What made him do it?"

"I told him your story," Carter said, his chin up. He looked around at her family. "And how the Grahams never left your side, and how they got a miracle."

"We sure did." Bryce's mother leaned her head on Bryce's shoulder. "We sure did."

When Bryce pushed away her plate, her dad got up from his chair. "Are you ready?"

"I guess." Bryce laughed.

Her mom handed her a sweater. They were going out back.

Carter discreetly helped Bryce down the stairs, his hand around her waist. As they passed through the basement doors, she shivered. It was an unusually cold October day.

"Ugh," Sydney said as they walked, folding her arms over her chest, where the word DUBSTEP was printed in neon pink. "Why won't winter stay away?"

They came to the barn. Maybe Bryce's present was more power tools. Thanks to Bryce and her dad, and sometimes Carter, the barn was no longer just patched up, it was transformed.

Bryce's dad bypassed the door, however, and they followed him toward the pasture.

As they came around the barn, Bryce's eyes fell on a familiar-looking blue tarp. They had pulled the half-finished plane out of the barn when they started work, but Bryce hadn't laid eyes on it since then. Her dad pulled the tarp away with a flourish, like a magician revealing a trick. "Ta-da!"

The old two-seater looked pristine, not a bolt out of place. It had been painted deep cherry red, facing a thin landing strip mowed through the dry grass.

"You finished it," Bryce said in awe.

"I helped," Sydney said proudly.

"I thought you were doing your homework," Bryce teased, punching her sister on the arm. She smiled at the thought of her sister and her dad handing each other tools, laying out tape for the paint.

"That too." Sydney rolled her eyes.

"Alrighty. Let's do it," Mike said, taking two pairs of aviator goggles out of his pockets. Everyone turned to Bryce. She watched her sister's eyes land on the plane, and back to her.

"Sydney should go," Bryce decided.

"Really?" her father asked.

"Yeah. Sydney gets first ride for her painting job. And her excellent secret-keeping."

"I mean, I don't have to." Sydney fidgeted.

"No, come on, Syd," Bryce urged. "You know you want to wear those goggles."

"It's true." Sydney grinned and climbed into the plane with their father.

Bryce, her mother, and Carter all stood to the side of the landing strip as Sydney and her father took off. The little plane kicked up dust, sped down the runway, lifting up just yards before the tree line, heading due east as it started to soar. From the ground, they all began to cheer.

Bryce closed her eyes and thought of her father and sister. Through their eyes, she saw it: the hills where the grass was burned gold, the flaming red trees. She heard them whoop at the top of their lungs. And then, like a jewel nestled inside the valleys, she saw the twirling green of a river. The Cumberland? No. The Mississippi.

Through her closed eyes the colors of the landscape bended and looped through one another like ribbons. Whirling through the air, over, under, the water glistening bright. She could hear her father and Sydney shouting and laughing at each other. Bryce opened her eyes.

Finally the plane circled back around and landed, not exactly gracefully, but in one piece.

Bryce's father hopped out first and then helped Sydney, whose hair was tousled from the wind, her cheeks flushed pink.

"Who's next?" he said. "Beth?"

"I don't know, I already did my hair," Bryce's mother said, patting it down. Bryce's father knit his brow.

"Oh, I'm kidding!" she cried. She laughed and climbed in, repeating, "Oh, brother, oh, brother," as she struggled to wiggle the goggles into place.

As he helped his wife into the tiny seat, Bryce's father turned back to them with a wink. "See you kids back at the house. Your mom and I might be a while."

Bryce's mother blushed and gave a wave. "Ignore your father."

Bryce and Sydney watched their plane take flight, soaring through the sky. She kept her face turned up, squinting whenever the sun broke through the thick clouds.

She heard her father's laughter, her mother's squeals, and caught her sister's eyes, shining as she shivered in the chilly morning. Sydney tucked her arms into her T-shirt, and Bryce put a hand on her sister's shoulder, rubbing it to warm her up. They were together. They were happy.

This was where she belonged.

CHAPTER THIRTY-FOUR

I t warmed up later that day, warm enough to see a movie at Big Chief Drive-In. The feature that night was *The Searchers*. Carter would admit to nothing, saying it was the best coincidence in the world.

The day after Bryce's birthday it got even warmer, almost hot. Toward evening Carter and Bryce took a trip to Percy Lake, both of them whooping like wild dogs on the big hill. They tucked into the trees and bushes covered in the flames of change, breaking into the clearing, breathing in the sickeningly sweet smell of past-ripe crabapples.

Leaves flew up in the wind, taking little dips to land

on Bryce's dress, then diving off the bluff into the green-patched lake.

They sat watching the sun set, dissolving to ooze orange in the trees, like an egg yolk in water. Bryce curled up next to Carter, leaning her head on his chest.

"Tell me something," she said. She did this a lot, when she got bored of the quiet. He usually pulled out some random fact about tendons or neurons.

"Okay. Here's something you don't know." He stroked her hair. "I was there the day you got hurt at the Trials."

"Really?" Bryce lifted her head to look at him. "Why?"

He shook his head. "I don't know. It was totally random. I was about to be a freshman at Vanderbilt, and I didn't know anybody yet—I had arrived early and I was wandering around campus, checking it out. The door to the natatorium was propped open and I heard cheering, so I went inside. And I saw this beautiful girl, standing on a platform in a swimsuit, so naturally . . ."

"So you saw me get hurt?" Bryce felt a little stab in her gut. *Why didn't you save me?*

"I didn't see the dive. I was distracted by something . . . but then I heard people gasp."

She shook off the wounded feeling. Carter was just a guy in the stands. But it was such a coincidence. "And then you found out I was at the same hospital as your brother."

"A few years later, yeah."

"Huh," Bryce said, her head back on Carter's chest. There was nothing else to be said about it. Stranger things had happened.

"Want to know something else?" he whispered after a while.

"Yes," she said.

"I wanted to kiss you the first day you brought me here."

Bryce answered him by doing just that, so long they had to come up for breath, and then leaned in for more.

The kisses sent spurts of fire down her back and sides, good fire, fire that licked with warmth in winter, melting ice into little wet pools. His hands ran up and down her bare arms, to her neck, her chest.

They were under the branches now, Bryce's back against the trunk of the tree, Carter's weight pressed against her. They slid down, locked by each other's arms, landing in the grass side by side.

Her breaths coming in quick bursts, Bryce met Carter's eyes, moving down to his nose, to his lips, to the buttons of his shirt.

She unbuttoned them.

Carter reached behind her neck to unzip her dress.

Bryce unbuckled his belt.

He unhooked her bra.

They undid each other.

Soon she was no longer Bryce Graham with the extraordinary head, the weak legs, the awkward hands. She was inside all that. By the look on Carter's face, he knew it, too. Their lives weren't in all the funny external gestures, the hands on skin, the lips on skin, one skeleton against the other, one mouth on the other mouth, the flesh hot, the arched back. It wasn't that.

With Carter, the root of everything was inside. The branches in autumn above her, his head in the crook of her shoulder, Bryce saw the root of everything.

Our lives come from the inside.

"I love you," he said into the night, his chest no longer heaving. They had wiggled back into their clothes. The chill had come back when the sun went down, and they were covered in sweat.

"I love you, too," Bryce said, but her breath was still ragged.

Her ears were ringing, morphing seamlessly into a familiar chorus of buzzing.

"Huh," she said.

"What?" Carter said quietly beside her.

"Bit late for cicadas," she said.

"I don't hear any," Carter said, his voice fading. "Just gonna rest my eyes for a bit," he said, soon followed by the steady, slow breaths of sleep.

"Okay," Bryce said, and stood up. The buzzing grew louder, as loud as it could ever get in late July. But it was October. Pain was rising from places it had never come from before—behind her ears, the base of her neck near her shoulders, shooting across her forehead.

She thought about rousing Carter, but another wave brought her to her knees, then to the ground in a crawling position.

Bryce started to list all the things she knew about the ground, to keep from passing out.

Hard dirt.

Blades of grass.

Broken acorn shells.

Twigs.

Soft sand.

Water lapping on the back of her hand.

That's not right! Bryce pushed up, angry that she had been tricked. Her brain was tricking her. Fear rose along with another wave of pain. She was no longer in control.

Speckled heat and light.

Back to the dark.

Gold light on the surface of the water.

Bryce's head throbbed, her lungs full of cotton, but at least she could stand.

"Oh," she realized with a hoarse whisper. She knew somehow, by the darkness darker than any she'd ever seen. By the way the water looked gold, like it was reversed with the sky. It never looked like that. Tonight was it. The vision she had seen. The dive. Her beginning, her end.

Bryce had almost convinced herself that it was all a mistake, that she was going to live. Not forever, just long enough to do more things. To go to college. To be in love for a long time. To travel the world. She felt her face contort as if she was going to cry, but she didn't know if she physically could.

She was answered with pain so heavy it brought her back into darkness. She fought her way out like she was being buried in the air.

Bryce stepped as carefully as she could to Carter, fast asleep, and kissed him gently so as not to wake him. Would he be surprised to find her gone in the morning? Bryce wondered if he had started believing she would live, too.

As she made her way to the edge of the bluff, holding saplings for balance, Bryce said silent good-byes to her mother, her father, her little sister. She could picture them in their beds: her mother in her electric-pink bathrobe; her dad snoring in a sweat suit, a biography of a baseball player open on his chest; Sydney as Bryce had seen her the last couple of nights, her face buried in a book about music theory.

The buzzing was too loud now to make out any other sounds, and pain was bursting behind her eyes like a fireworks finale. With every inch of movement her muscles had left, Bryce crossed her hands in front of her in perfect form, bent her legs, tense and steady, and sprung off. A tuck in the dark, then toward the light, straight as an arrow. A last dive into forever.

ACKNOWLEDGMENTS

Thank you to my hard-working parents, Brad and Sharon, whose simultaneous high standards and sense of humor have filled my world with purpose. And to my brothers, Wyatt and Dylan, who have been calling me on my b.s. since I was out of the womb, and will do so forever. I hope my extended family, the Rundes and the Averys, will see this book's reverence for the American countryside, which has grown out of my time spent with them in their various home states.

Emma and Mandy, all the characters are you at some point. I hope your copies get covered in the dust from wherever you are. Rhett: for many more reasons than why I got to write this book, I'm glad our stars aligned.

Thank you to the staff of Nina's Coffee Café of Saint Paul, who provided me with food, drink, and an office for days on end, and who didn't judge my surly demeanor and haggard appearance too much.

An enormous debt of gratitude to my editor, Joelle Hobeika, for her guidance as I made my way through my first novel, and her patience, which allowed me to feel I was taking advice from a good friend. Another grateful nod to Laura Schreiber, Emily Meehan, and the whole Hyperion team. Their contributions brought this novel to another dimension, and they have taught me more than they know. Thank you to Southpaw Entertainment, for the inspiration and encouragement.

On that note, thank you to everyone at Alloy Entertainment for this opportunity. Truly, they have changed my life.